DOOM AND BROOM

A SPELLBOUND PARANORMAL COZY MYSTERY, BOOK 2

ANNABEL CHASE

RED PALM PRESS LLC

Doom and Broom

A Spellbound Paranormal Cozy Mystery, Book 2

By Annabel Chase

Sign up for my newsletter here http://eepurl.com/ctYNzf and or like me on Facebook so you can find out about new releases.

Cover Design by Alchemy

❀ Created with Vellum

CHAPTER 1

"TODAY BEGINS a new chapter for our newest student," Professor Holmes said. "I know we will all enjoy watching her pass this milestone."

Only if they enjoyed vomit.

We stood in the middle of a field on the outskirts of town—five remedial witches and the kindly Professor Holmes from the Arabella St. Simon's Academy, or the ASS Academy as I called it. The sky was a clear blue, so there was little chance of getting lost in a cloud. I stared at the broomstick in Begonia's hand, a sense of dread creeping through me. I wouldn't be eligible for my own broom until I passed the first phase of the class, not that I was in a hurry to have one. The only thing I intended to do with a broom was sweep.

Hesitantly, I raised my hand. "Professor? I don't have to ride alone today, right?"

"Not to worry, Miss Hart," he said. "You will have ample warning when the day arrives for your solo."

Begonia gripped my arm with far too much enthusiasm. "And then you get to go to Broomstix for your very own broom."

My stomach turned over at the thought.

"Now which one of you would like to take Miss Hart on her very first flight?" The professor's gaze swept across the other witches.

Technically, it wouldn't be my first flight, just my first flight on a broomstick. The honor of taking me on my first flight went to Daniel, the fallen angel who was the reason I was stuck in this town in the first place. When he flew me inside the town border, neither of us had any clue I wouldn't be able to get out again thanks to the curse that kept all supernatural residents trapped in Spellbound. It was a bad time to discover I was actually a witch.

Millie's hand shot up first. "I volunteer."

Professor Holmes smiled at her. "That's the kind of helpful attitude I like to see, Millie."

Millie whispered to me, "If I'm up there with you, I won't be in the danger zone."

Helpful, indeed.

"But I would rather you ride solo," the professor continued. "Begonia will partner with Miss Hart today."

Although Millie tried to mask her disappointment, she wasn't very good at it.

Professor Holmes addressed the group. "Now young witches, most of you will remember the basic tenets of broom flying from last term. Grip, balance, and focus."

Four heads bobbed in agreement. I listened intently, trying to absorb every word.

"Millie, I'd like you to go first and demonstrate," Professor Holmes said. "As I recall, you were our star pupil in this class. That's why I prefer for you to fly solo."

Millie stepped forward with her broom, smiling broadly. I didn't blame her for the self-satisfied grin. I'd be beaming like a maniac too if someone told me I was a star pupil of any witch training classes. So far, I was more like the village idiot.

Millie mounted her broom, two hands gripping the top end of the handle and her bottom shoved back toward the bristles.

"Do you need a running start or something?" I asked. How else did they get the brooms in the air?

The others giggled.

"No, silly," Begonia said. "You use a spell."

"Does everyone use the same spell?" I asked.

"There are standard spells one can use," Professor Holmes said. "But, as with any spell, a witch is free to personalize it. Embrace it as her own."

I liked the emphasis on individuality in the coven. There didn't seem to be the idea that every witch was the same. It was nice.

"Carry on, Millie," Professor Holmes said.

Millie straightened her shoulders, as much as one could straighten shoulders when hunched over a broomstick. She muttered a phrase under her breath.

Professor Holmes clapped his hands twice. "Louder, so we can all hear you. This is a learning exercise, remember?"

Millie cleared her throat. "If I want to touch the sky/then I need to get up high."

The broom began to rise. Millie's expression was serene. She clearly didn't suffer from the fear and anxiety that were my emotional staples.

"How does the spell work without her wand?" I asked.

Millie's broom stuttered to a halt. She turned to glare at me.

"You need to stop interrupting," Begonia whispered. "It breaks her concentration."

Oops. "Sorry," I said softly.

Professor Holmes sighed. "Emma's question is a good one. We should answer it first. In the case of broom flying, the broomstick itself acts as your wand. Each stick is imbued with magic. The witch simply activates this magic by focusing her will and using an incantation."

That made sense.

Millie glanced over her shoulder at us. "Can I go now?" she huffed.

Professor Holmes gave a crisp nod.

Millie repeated the spell, focusing her will. I watched as the broom rose higher and higher. When she was high enough to clear the trees, she lurched forward. The longer she was up there, the faster she rode. I could see why she was the star pupil—Millie was a natural. The crucial element seemed to be that she enjoyed it. With her hair streaming behind her and the sun shining on her face, she was in her element. I felt a pang of envy. Why couldn't I embrace flying with the same fervor?

"Well done, Millie," Professor Holmes called.

I doubted Millie could hear him. She continued to zip around in the air until, finally, Professor

Holmes sent her owl to intercept her. Now I understood why the owls attended broom practice. My spotted owl, Sedgwick, was with me. He was different from the other owls, which we discovered when I met him at Paws and Claws, the animal rescue center. Sedgwick was my familiar—it was a witch thing, apparently. The other witches in Spellbound had cats as companions and spiritual advisors, whereas I had a cantankerous owl. Lucky me.

Millie came gliding down to the ground like a pro and we all clapped heartily. I hoped my ride was as smooth as hers.

Laurel, the youngest witch in our class, was next to ride, followed by Sophie. I'd assumed Sophie would be the problem pupil during broomstick training. She was clumsy on a good day. To my surprise, she took to the sky with ease. Maybe it was just her wand that gave her trouble. Since she didn't need a wand to ride a broom, she performed much better.

My stomach clenched when I realized it was our turn.

"Should I sit in front of Begonia or behind her?" I asked. I recalled amusement park rides where the bigger person had to sit in a certain position relative to the smaller one. Maybe it was like that.

"You should probably start by sitting in front of your partner," Professor Holmes said. "That way she can keep you from slipping off."

Slipping off? Those are not the words I wanted to hear before riding a broom hundreds of feet in the air.

Begonia gently touched my shoulder. "Don't worry, Emma. Witches rarely slip off their broomstick."

The use of the word 'rarely' implied that they sometimes did. It didn't make me feel much better.

"Don't be nervous," Begonia said. "I'll be right there with you."

At least I trusted Begonia. Trust was important when someone was escorting you high in the air. Trust didn't stop me from vomiting, however.

Begonia straddled the back of the broom and gestured for me to sit in front of her. I swallowed hard.

"In case it becomes an issue," I said, "I would like a wake instead of a funeral. Lots of drinking and good food. And don't have it at Underkoffler's." Piotr Underkoffler was a creepy vampire as well as the owner of a funeral home in town. I didn't want to be left alone with him for a second, even as a corpse.

"Understood," Professor Holmes said. I detected a hint of a smile on his lips.

I threw one leg over the top of the broom and tried to settle on the narrow handle. I didn't see how this could possibly be comfortable. As a child, I'd struggled with any bicycle seat that wasn't in the shape of a banana.

"Remember," Professor Holmes said. "Grip, balance, and focus."

I paid close attention to the position of my hands on the broomstick. My knuckles were already white and we hadn't left the ground. I didn't know how to control balance, especially when I wasn't the only one on the broom. Begonia was going to act as our rudder. Her role was to steer and keep us afloat. My role was not to die.

"Do you want to try the spell?" Begonia asked.

"Maybe you should do it this time," I said. "I'll do the next one."

Begonia's voice was confident and clear. "Take us off the grassy ground/to where birdsong is the only sound."

I wondered if spells like this ever got misinterpreted. What if the magic assumed that she wanted to be sitting in a treetop near an eagles' nest? I preferred my spells to be more specific. Then again, maybe that was the lawyer in me talking. My spells would be something along the lines of *where the birdsong is the only sound, including but not limited to, the empty sky at least fifty feet from the ground or within a twenty-foot radius of cirrus clouds."*

The broom rose slowly and steadily. I felt my stomach dip and I was glad I'd opted to forgo breakfast beforehand. I squeezed my eyes shut.

"Your eyes are open, right?" Begonia asked. "That's a requirement."

"Wide open," I lied. There was no way I was opening my eyes right now. My stomach was relaying all of the information my body needed to know. My eyes would be no help whatsoever.

"It can be tricky with two people," Begonia said. "We all start out riding tandem, but we switch to solo as soon as we qualify."

So what was she trying to tell me? She was not as good on a broom now that I was here? I was hoping for a more confident statement.

The broom wobbled slightly and I gripped the handle harder, my nails digging into my skin. I was pretty sure I'd drawn blood. Not that I cared. I was more concerned with not falling off the broom and plummeting to the earth.

"Look," she exclaimed. "The harpies are out."

The harpies are out? What did that mean? Now I had to look or she would know that my eyes were closed. Slowly, I opened one eye just enough so that I could see. In the distance, I noticed three sets of wings. I couldn't determine whether they were ugly bird women or something else.

"Is it the Minor sisters?" I asked. The Minors lived in the house next door. They were a fearsome bunch, especially the grandmother, Octavia. Her tongue doubled as a skewer.

"Yes, can't you tell?"

Um, no. I'd only seen the harpies in their human forms. "Do they take their harpy forms often?"

"I've seen them appear a few times," Begonia said. "I think they like the fresh air."

It was like the werewolves and turning. The harpies embraced their natural state. Both groups tended to live in human form in Spellbound, but there was this whole other side to them. Seeing the harpies airborne now, I understood them a little bit better. On the ground, they were intimidating. In the air, however, I was in awe of them.

"Where's Sedgwick?" Begonia asked. "He should be up here. Mine is at nine o'clock."

I made the mistake of turning to look. The quick movement coupled with a glimpse of the ground below sent shockwaves through my system. I did the one thing I really, really hoped to avoid.

Bull's-eye, Sedgwick said, making his appearance. *You couldn't have done that better if you'd tried.*

I kept my eyes closed this time. I didn't need to look to know what I'd done.

"Professor?" I croaked.

And a few chunks on Millie, too. Sedgwick whistled. *She does not look happy about it.*

After an abrupt end to class, Begonia and I went directly to Mix-n-Match to find an anti-anxiety potion.

"Why not the apothecary?" I asked.

"Too many members of the coven lurking there," Begonia whispered. "We don't want to draw attention to your issue."

"Don't witches run both places?" I queried.

"Mix-n-Match is co-owned by a fairy," she explained. "We don't tend to hang out there as much."

The shop window was decorated with colorful bottles that looked like they were filled with either genies or perfume.

"I can see the fairy influence," I said, as we entered the shop.

"Oh good," Begonia said. "Paisley's working today. She's one of us."

"Hey Begonia," Paisley said. "I haven't seen you in a couple of weeks."

"I've been super busy with school and my new friend. This is Emma Hart."

Paisley's eyes lit up at the sight of me. "The new witch." She seemed mildly awestruck and I felt a little like Harry Potter during his first trip to Diagon Alley. I suppose if you're trapped in the same town for the rest of your extended or immortal life, a new resident is a big deal.

"That's me," I said.

Another young woman stepped out from behind the counter. She didn't sport any wings, so I ruled out fairy. Must be another witch.

"And how is remedial witchcraft, Begonia?" she asked.

I took an instant dislike to her, probably because of her snotty tone and the way she emphasized 'remedial.'

"Classes have gotten a lot livelier since Emma arrived," Begonia said. Thankfully, she opted not to mention today's mishap.

"I don't doubt it." The other witch came closer to inspect me. She looked about my age with an aquiline nose, thin eyebrows, and a long, slender neck that was more reminiscent of a giraffe than a graceful swan. "They haven't figured out which coven you *really* belong to yet, have they?"

"Jemima, don't be awful," Paisley said. "You know perfectly well her coven is here with us now."

Jemima sniffed. "I hear your familiar is an owl." She pronounced the word 'owl' with such derision, I half expected a parliament of owls to swoop in and peck out her eyes.

I glanced toward the door and sighed. No such luck. "Yes," I said. "Sedgwick is my familiar and he's wonderful." Actually, he was a moody thorn in my side, but I'd never admit it to the judgmental witch in front of me.

"We're here for a potion, Jemima," Begonia said. "Why don't you let Paisley help us and go back to regrowing your eyebrows?"

Jemima's mouth formed a thin line. "That was one time, Begonia Spence, and you know it. My eyebrows are fine now." Her finger flew to touch the arched shape of her thin eyebrow. Reassurance.

"If you say so," Begonia said airily and Jemima stomped off to the back of the shop.

"Is she always like that?" I asked, once the witch was out of earshot.

Paisley bit back a laugh. "Pretty much. What can I help you find?"

"Emma is learning how to fly on a broomstick," Begonia explained. "She needs something to calm her stomach."

"And my nerves," I added.

Paisley studied me. "You're afraid of heights?"

"Very."

"Well, that's a first for a witch." She began examining the bottles on the shelf. "I didn't mean that to sound judgmental. I'm just surprised."

"That's okay," I said. I knew I presented the coven with a lot of questions, like which coven I was descended from and what my abilities were. We were still figuring it all out. So far, we knew my mother had been a witch but little else. She drowned when I was three. I had no clue whether she knew she was a witch. I could speak telepathically with my owl but not a cat, like the witches of this coven. And I was deathly afraid of heights.

"So you need something to settle your stomach and also to prevent you from having a panic attack on the broom?" Paisley pulled three bottles from the shelf and placed them on the counter. "It can be trial and error with potions, I'm afraid. You'll need to test each one for a couple of days and see how your body reacts."

I looked at the colorful liquids floating in the bottles. "Which one do you recommend I try first?"

Paisley touched the top of the bottle with orange liquid. "This one tastes the worst but is usually the most effective."

Not much different from the human world then. "And it will help with both issues?"

"Well, it's an anti-anxiety potion, so it should help with the fear of heights, which should then reduce the likelihood of nausea and vomiting."

"Any potential side effects?" Begonia asked.

Paisley gave me a sheepish look. "Nausea and vomiting."

Begonia patted my back. "The key word is *potential*."

"I'll try it." I didn't have much of a choice.

"Take it for a week," Paisley advised. "If you're not seeing the results you want, then try the next potion."

I stared at the orange goo. "This is not going to be fun."

"Do you want to take the other two now, just to have them accessible at home?" Paisley asked.

"I think I'll wait," I said. "It feels more optimistic to leave them here."

"Agreed," Begonia said.

"How much do I owe you?" I asked.

Begonia stopped me from reaching into my handbag. "The coven is paying, Emma. They see it as a worthwhile expense."

"In that case, you mean Professor Holmes is paying," I said.

She pretended to find something interesting on the nearest shelf. "The coven is my official answer."

I took my orange medicine in a nondescript brown bag and we headed out for lunch.

CHAPTER 2

FOLLOWING a leisurely lunch with Begonia at Toadstools, I decided to stop by Petals, the flower shop. Gareth, my ghost vampire roommate and former owner of my house, had requested that I restock his favorite flowers.

"You're that new witch, aren't you?" the owner said. I knew from Begonia that her name was Sybil.

"Emma Hart," I said. "It's nice to meet you. My friends tell me you're a dryad."

"I'm an ash tree nymph," she said, "We're called the Meliae. Technically, dryads are only oak tree nymphs."

Oops. "Sorry," I said.

She waved me off. "A common mistake. I hear you've taken over Gareth's role as the public defender now."

"I needed a job here. I was a lawyer in the human world, so it wasn't too much of a stretch." Except for the fact that I'd never practiced criminal law and knew nothing about the laws of Spellbound.

"Terrible news about Jolene, isn't it?" Sybil said. "I hope you won't be needing to defend someone for her murder."

I froze. A murder? "Who's Jolene?"

"Werewolf," Sybil said. "So you haven't heard then." She seemed heartened to discover she was the harbinger of terrible news. "Poor dear is dead. She was found this morning in her house."

I continued to select an assortment of roses, careful not to prick my fingers on the thorns. "That's awful. What happened?"

"Don't know," she replied. "I heard the sheriff is talking to friends and loved ones now."

"Was she elderly?" I asked.

"Oh no," Sybil said with a dismissive wave. "A pretty young thing, about to get married to Alex."

"Who's Alex?"

She laughed. "You really don't know anybody, do you? Alex is a rising star of the pack." She lowered her voice. "Some see him as the natural successor to Lorenzo."

I wondered if Lorenzo knew this. I didn't think

I'd be happy to discover members of my pack were prematurely planning my replacement.

"You live in Gareth's old house, don't you?" she queried.

"I do."

"Thought so." She inclined her head toward the flowers in my hand. "He used to choose the same ones."

"Really?" I feigned surprise. "What a coincidence."

"Is it?" She peered at me and I wondered if she knew the truth, that I could see and hear Gareth's ghost. "What kind of witch are you anyway? I heard you're not from the same coven as the witches in Spellbound."

Well, she was very forward. "I don't know anything about my coven. I didn't know I was a witch until the council told me."

"I heard it was that wayward angel that lured you here," she said, carefully arranging tulips in a vase.

"Daniel didn't lure me here," I replied. "The whole thing was an accident." I thought he needed my help and I did something stupid. Got out of my car and ran toward a lake, waving my arms like a lunatic. "He saved me from certain death." I would have either drowned after jumping into the lake because I couldn't swim or my car would have run me over.

"He used to come in here to buy flowers for Elsa Knightsbridge."

"The mayor's daughter?"

"Mm. And that redheaded witch, too."

"Meg?" I'd met Meg my first day in town. She hadn't seemed happy to know Daniel was within shouting distance.

She smiled. "So maybe you know a few people after all."

"I haven't met the mayor's daughter," I said. "Only the mayor."

She whistled. "Truth be told, that Elsa is a piece of work. I don't know why everyone was so surprised when he dumped her. I was surprised he started up with her in the first place."

"People can't always help who they fall in love with," I said.

"It's with whom they fall in love," she corrected me. "Don't they teach grammar in the human world anymore?"

"Standards are sliding," I admitted. "As long as we're understood, though, what's the harm?"

She shook her head, disappointment etched in her smooth features. "Anything besides the roses?"

"Yes, a bouquet of those yellow flowers. They look cheerful."

"They clash with the roses," she said.

"That's okay," I said. "They're not for me. I'm going to bring them to Alex and his family."

She raised a skeptical eyebrow. "You're a strange one all right. You said you don't know him."

"Do I need to know him to express sorrow for his loss? Don't they teach empathy in Spellbound anymore?"

She considered me for a moment. "Alex lives in the Pines. Head due west out of town and you'll run straight into it."

"How much do I owe you?"

"No charge today. Gareth was a loyal customer. I expect you'll be as well."

"Thank you."

"You're welcome." She gave me a curt nod. "Nice to know the standard for manners hasn't gone downhill, too."

Lorenzo Mancini stood in front of Jolene and Alex's house in his finely tailored suit. I recognized the alpha of the werewolf pack from the council meeting in the Great Hall, where it was determined that I'd move into Gareth's house and take over his job. Lorenzo was deep in conversation with a centaur, Sheriff Hugo, the town's leader of law enforcement. The sheriff and I got a chance to know each other during the investigation into Gareth's murder when I was accused of overstepping my boundaries. Needless to say, he wasn't my biggest fan.

Lorenzo sniffed the air and turned toward me as I approached. "Miss Hart. I thought I picked up an unfamiliar scent."

Sheriff Hugo grunted in my general direction. "What brings you out to this neck of the woods, Miss Hart?"

I held up the bouquet of yellow flowers. "I wanted to express my condolences to Alex."

"What a thoughtful gesture," Lorenzo said. "He's inside with his family."

Werewolves were everywhere. I was surprised the sheriff hadn't cordoned off the house as a crime scene. The front door was open, so I went inside. I identified Alex immediately. He was being consoled by an older woman, possibly his mother. The woman turned and glared at me.

"You're not a member of the pack," she said. Her

eyes glistened with unshed tears. "What are you doing here?"

I hesitated. Now that I was here, I felt stupid. "I was in town when I heard the news about Jolene. I wanted to offer my condolences."

Alex lifted his head and looked at me. He noticed the bouquet in my hand. "Are those for me?"

I nodded and stuck out my hand. "I'm sorry," I said. "I don't know what the protocol is here for showing sympathy. This is what people do where I'm from."

"Werewolves don't give *flowers*," the woman snarled.

Alex accepted the bouquet and handed it to the woman. "Would you be so kind as to put these in water? One death in my house today is quite enough."

She bowed her head, a submissive gesture, and disappeared into the kitchen.

"Alex Ricci," he said. "You must be the new witch."

"Emma Hart," I said. "I didn't mean to intrude."

"No, no." He wiped the tears from his red-rimmed eyes. "It's a nice gesture. I appreciate it." He tilted his head in the direction of the kitchen. "Please excuse my mother. She's grieving also. She loved Jolene like a daughter."

I didn't ask any questions. The lost look in his eyes told me he was still processing her death.

"I won't take up any more of your time," I said. "I just wanted to say how sorry I am."

"Thank you, Emma."

I hurried out of the house before his mother returned. The front porch was overflowing with bodies and I tried to nudge my way through them. Before I made it to the steps, the sound of sobbing drew my attention to the far end of the porch. The crowd parted just enough to reveal a girl on the porch swing. With her long, blond hair and unblemished skin, she looked no older than seventeen. She appeared distraught, her eyes red and swollen and her cheeks stained with tears.

"Is she hurt?" I asked aloud.

"Not hurt. Just hurtin'," a man said. "That's Kayla. She's the one who found Jolene."

Poor thing. She'd be forever scarred by a single moment. "Younger sister?" I asked.

"Jolene's cousin. She'd been fighting with her own parents, so Jolene had taken her in. She'd always been like a big sister to her."

And now she was gone. Although I didn't have

siblings, I'd lost my mother and father at a young age. I knew that kind of grief intimately—the loss of someone you loved and looked up to.

"I'm going to see if she's okay," I said. It seemed like the adults were preoccupied with comforting each other and Kayla had been brushed aside.

I threaded my way through the bodies until I reached the porch swing. Kayla glanced up at me, her brown eyes shining.

"Anyone sitting here?" I asked.

Wordlessly, she shook her head. I plopped down beside her and gently pushed against the floor with my feet so the swing moved. I'd always taken comfort in rocking motions.

"I don't know you," the girl said.

"Emma Hart," I replied. "I'm new in town."

Her brow lifted slightly. "The witch?"

I nodded. "How are you holding up? I heard you're the one who found Jolene."

Kayla sniffed and drew her knees to her chest. "Found her on the kitchen floor. I'd only been in the shower for about five minutes."

"Had you seen her at all this morning?"

"'Course. It was the same as any other morning. Alex left for work. I went downstairs and ate breakfast, then brought Jolene a cup of coffee."

"In her bedroom?"

Kayla nodded. "Jolene's been a late riser as long as I've known her. Sometimes she doesn't want to get up..." She trailed off. "Anyway, I got into the habit of bringing her coffee to try and drag her butt out of bed. Been working too."

"So after you stopped by her room and went into the shower, she went downstairs to the kitchen. Is that typical?"

"Not really. She usually hung around in bed a while longer, reading or doing a crossword. By the time I'd get out of the shower, she was still in her room."

"But not today?"

"No. She went downstairs. I guess to get her breakfast." She paused. "I thought maybe *he* was coming by again."

"Who's *he*?"

"Same as I told the alpha and Sheriff Hugo," she said. "That angel I used to see skulking around here after Alex went to work."

"Angel?" I echoed. There was only one angel I knew of in Spellbound.

"Daniel Starr." She gave me a hesitant glance. "You know him, don't you? I heard he trapped you here."

"He didn't trap me," I said. Not on purpose. "What do you mean that he was skulking around?"

Kayla shrugged. "You must've heard about his reputation by now."

Daniel's history was difficult to avoid. I seemed to encounter bitter women everywhere I turned in Spellbound.

"From what I understand, Daniel's affairs were quite some time ago." And much to my dismay, he'd sworn off the opposite sex right in front of me only a couple of weeks ago. He viewed the sacrifice as his shot at redemption.

"I'm not saying they were definitely bumping uglies, but they seemed mighty comfortable with one another. If I were Alex, I wouldn't have liked it one bit."

"Did you ever mention Daniel's visits to Alex?" I asked in a low voice. I didn't want anyone to hear me asking questions, not after Sheriff Hugo's multiple warnings the last time I got involved in a case. But this was *Daniel* she was talking about. I couldn't let it go. I felt a sense of obligation to him, and probably a few other emotions I pushed down and ignored.

Kayla plucked at a loose piece of wood on the seat of the swing. "I didn't, but now I'm wondering if I should have done."

A shadow fell over us and I recognized its owner without so much as a glance at his hooves.

"Is this witch bothering you, Kayla?"

"No, Sheriff," Kayla replied. "We were just getting to know each other."

Sheriff Hugo narrowed his eyes at me. "Don't you have a training class to go to? Maybe learn to wield that wand of yours without injuring others."

He was right. I had an afternoon class with the head witch, Lady Weatherby. She already seemed to dislike me. It would not be a smart move to show up late.

I gave Kayla a quick pat on the leg. "Take care of yourself. If you need someone to talk to…"

"If she needs someone to talk, that's what the pack is for." Lorenzo appeared beside the sheriff. "As I was just explaining to Sheriff Hugo, the pack can handle this matter just fine without interference."

I resisted the urge to smile. "You mean you're kicking the sheriff off the case?"

"Mr. Mancini knows perfectly well he doesn't have the right to do that," the sheriff said.

"And Sheriff Hugo knows perfectly well that pack matters are not covered by the town charter."

"We don't know that this is a pack matter…"

Sheriff Hugo began, but Lorenzo held up a hand to silence him.

"Jolene was a member of the werewolf pack. She was found in her own home on pack land."

The sheriff tried again. "But we don't know yet..."

"Until there is evidence to the contrary, your work here is done," Lorenzo said.

"What about the body?" I asked. "Can the pack handle an autopsy?"

Lorenzo's eyes flashed gold. "You have no business here, Miss Hart. If and when there's someone to defend, we'll let you know."

There was nothing more for me to say, so I excused myself and vacated pack premises.

CHAPTER 3

CLASS WAS IN FIFTEEN MINUTES, so I summoned Sedgwick. It was the fastest way to send an urgent message to Daniel.

You rang, my lady. Sedgwick appeared above me, flapping his wings and giving me his usual look of disdain.

"Stop pretending to be a butler," I said.

Stop pretending to be a witch.

Hardy har. "I need you to take a message to Daniel."

Can you write it down? He doesn't speak owl.

I glanced around helplessly for an inkwell and paper. Not the kind of thing one tends to carry around.

"Just show up at his house," I said irritably. "He'll figure out that I need to see him."

Sedgwick rolled his golden eyes. *Fine, Your Majesty. Where does he live?*

I faltered. "Um, I actually don't know." I'd only ever seen him at my house or in town. And the lake, of course. The place where my life changed forever.

You go try not to die in class. I'll figure it out.

"You make me miss my phone for so many reasons," I said. Mostly because my phone never talked back.

Sedgwick flew off and I hurried to the academy, arriving with only seconds to spare.

"Miss Hart, so glad you could join us." Lady Weatherby stood in the front of the class when I burst through the doors, panting and looking like an escaped mental patient.

I slipped into the end seat next to Laurel.

"Today we will be tackling practical spells," Lady Weatherby said. "Can anyone name one of them?"

Millie's hand was first in the air.

"Yes, Millie?"

"A water spell, a light spell, a summoning spell, and an unlocking spell." She folded her arms and smiled triumphantly.

Lady Weatherby cleared her throat. "Or four of them."

"I was going to say a summoning spell," Laurel mumbled.

"And which one of you would like to demonstrate the light spell?" Lady Weatherby asked.

Every hand shot up except mine. I had no clue how to do any of those spells. I was still practicing the basic defensive spells.

"Laurel, step up here and show Miss Hart how to do a light spell. It is, after all, one of the most useful spells we do."

Laurel bounced out of her seat and hustled to the front of the room. She held her wand vertically and closed her eyes. "Bless me with sight/bring forth the light."

The tip of her wand glowed with a pale light.

"Well done, Laurel. Can anyone offer words of improvement?"

Millie's hand waved in the air again. "She closed her eyes. You should never close your eyes when performing a spell."

So that rule applied off the broom as well. Good to know, although I wasn't sure how Lady Weatherby could have seen that Laurel's eyes were closed since she was facing us.

"Miss Hart, why don't you give it a try? I have a feeling this is a spell even you can do."

Gee, thanks for the vote of confidence, I thought to myself.

That wasn't a vote of confidence, Sedgwick said. *She thinks you can't do it.*

I shot a death glare at my owl, now at the back of the room. *Thank you, Captain Obvious. I was being sarcastic.*

In that case, you must try harder. I am fluent in sarcasm and I failed to detect your tone.

Did you find Daniel?

He flew behind me into town.

I hoped no one got to him before I did.

I stepped up to the front of the room and held my wand vertically, as Laurel had done. Then I focused my will.

"Out of the darkness and into the light," I said. The tip of my wand glowed a brilliant white.

Applause erupted.

"But she didn't use a rhyme," Millie howled in protest.

"Settle down, witches," Lady Weatherby said. "I have said before the rhyme is not always necessary. As long as the will is strong, you can achieve results."

Inwardly, I was beaming. I had no idea why I chose not to do a rhyme. The incantation just came to me. I was relieved that it didn't backfire. The last thing I needed was to extinguish every fey lantern in town.

Millie raised her chin. "Lady Weatherby, may I please try without using a rhyme?"

"You've shown off quite enough for one day Millie," Lady Weatherby said.

I bit back a smile. I liked Millie, but I had to admit that I enjoyed hearing Lady Weatherby put her in her place. This was supposed to be the remedial class. We should all suck equally.

"While you're up here," Lady Weatherby said to me. "Why don't you try a water spell?"

"What does a water spell do?" I asked. Although it seemed self-explanatory, I wanted to be sure before I performed the spell.

"Laurel, you may tell Miss Hart the effect of a water spell," Lady Weatherby said.

"Water sprays from the tip of your wand like a hose," Laurel said. "It's handy in a fire."

"Couldn't it be used as a defensive spell?" I asked.

"Any spell can be used as a defensive spell," Lady Weatherby said. "But these spells lean toward the practical. If you are lost in the mountains, for example, and you need water."

"I can drink from my wand," I finished for her.

Knowing that water would spout from the top, I wasn't sure in what position to hold the wand. If I held it vertically, it would rain back down on my head. If I pointed it at anyone else, it would douse her. Lady Weatherby seemed to sense my apprehension.

"There is a bin at the back of the room," she said. "Aim for that."

I stepped over to the left so that the bin was in my direct line of sight. I extended my wand and said, "Wand let the water zoom/to the bin across the room."

The water formed a perfect arc as it streamed into the bin. I couldn't believe it. I was on a roll today. I turned and flashed Lady Weatherby a proud smile.

"Good," Lady Weatherby said. She didn't return the smile. "Why don't you see if you can complete a summoning spell?"

"What am I summoning? Something in the room or not in the room?"

"If you're within range," Laurel said, "you can just point the wand and the item will come to you. If you can't see it, you have to think hard about it and do the right incantation."

"What's the right incantation?" I asked.

"As always, that is a matter of trial and error," Lady Weatherby said.

Fabulous. "Doesn't matter what I summon?"

"I vote for a hot guy," Begonia said.

Lady Weatherby narrowed her eyes. "There will be no summoning of residents. Items only. You know the rules, Begonia."

Begonia's cheeks reddened.

What would be the easiest thing to summon? Pencil? No, of course not. There were no pencils in Spellbound. An article of clothing? No. It was probably best to summon an item in the room. Don't overreach.

I surveyed the classroom. My gaze alighted on a ceramic rabbit on a shelf in the back of the room. I pointed my wand and said, "Leave the shelf bare/bring forth the hare."

The ceramic rabbit remained on the shelf. I looked at Lady Weatherby over my shoulder. That quickly, one of the witches screamed in horror. I turned back to see the hair on Millie growing at an exponential rate. Not just the hair on her head. Hair was growing out of every follicle of her body. It slid down and covered her clothes like vines. Her beard extended to the floor—she made circus freaks look like freshly scrubbed army recruits.

"Uh oh," I said. "What did I do?"

Lady Weatherby pressed her lips together. I recognized the gesture as her effort not to show annoyance. It wasn't working.

"You said to bring forth the hair, so it did," she said.

"H-a-r-e, like the rabbit," I said.

"Spells do not always distinguish between homonyms," Lady Weatherby said. "You must take care when choosing your words."

"Can someone please fix me?" Millie's voice was muffled by the layers of hair.

I looked at Lady Weatherby, waiting for her to snap her fingers and correct my error.

"Get to it, Miss Hart," the head witch said. "Your classmate is counting on you."

I stared at the bearded wonder that was once Millie.

"If you can't change her back, we can always introduce her to George," Begonia said, stifling a giggle.

"Who's George?" I asked. The name sounded vaguely familiar.

"The Yeti," Laurel said and burst into laughter.

"You always said you wanted to grow your hair

down your back," Sophie added, barely containing herself.

"Fff...ot...unny," the hairball said.

"What's that?" I asked.

"Millie said it's not funny," Lady Weatherby interpreted. "And I concur. Please correct your mistake, Miss Hart. We don't have all day."

I tapped my wand against my chin, thinking. "Okay, I think I've got it." I pointed my wand at Millie and said, "You look better bare/get rid of the hair."

I was optimistic as the hair began to recede—until it continued to recede. And then her eyebrows disappeared. Warning bells clanged.

Millie shrieked as her hands cupped her bald head. "What is wrong with you?"

"I'm so sorry," I said. She looked like the love child of a mole rat and an alien. "Let me try again."

Millie was lost in a haze of distress. "I don't even have eyelashes right now. What if a piece of dust hits my eye? I have no defenses."

"I can get rid of any dust particles," Laurel said and picked up her wand. "I clean my house all the time. My dad has allergies."

Lady Weatherby held up a hand. "No more spells,

Laurel. Not until Miss Hart has figured out a way to undo her mistake."

The pressure was on. The mature part of me understood what Lady Weatherby was doing. Like kids, new witches needed to learn how to clean up their own messes. The immature part of me, however, felt singled out and humiliated. I struggled to convince myself that Lady Weatherby had my best interests at heart, that she was only trying to make me the best witch I could be.

I held out my wand again and said, "Fix my newbie mistake/for my friend Millie's sake."

The hair sprouted on her head and grew back to its normal length. Her eyebrows reappeared and I assumed the rest of the hair I couldn't see was restored as well. I'd leave it for Millie to check later.

"You did it," Laurel cried. She seemed to be the only one overjoyed by my achievement.

"Take your seat, Miss Hart," Lady Weatherby said. No pat on the back for me.

"You are *so* getting your own voodoo doll," Millie hissed at me as I took my seat.

I'd been introduced to the voodoo dolls a few weeks ago, when my classmates shared their secret hideout with me. It was a place they went to get away from the coven and take out their frustrations —hence the voodoo dolls.

My face paled. Millie was my friend. I didn't want her to be angry with me.

"I'll make it up to you," I said in a low tone. I tried to think of something I had to offer and came up empty-handed. It was a horrible feeling—to realize how useless I was. I doubted Millie planned to commit a crime anytime soon, so my legal services weren't an option.

"Just do us both a favor and keep your distance," she said, still seething.

My stomach tensed. I didn't like people to be upset with me. I was a helper by nature and I took it hard when I managed to make things worse.

Laurel patted my hand. "Don't worry. It'll blow over."

I hoped she was right. Only five of us were remedial ASSes. I didn't want to be the source of any tension in such a small group.

When class drew to a close, I bolted before Millie could threaten me with bodily harm, not that I thought she would. She was a good person, just a very annoyed good person.

"Wait up, Emma," Begonia called. She caught up

with me before I crossed the road toward the town square.

"That was a nightmare," I said.

"Millie will cool off. I promise. She tries to act like the grown-up in our group, but she's totally not."

Her comment made me think of Kayla. With the discovery of her cousin's dead body, she'd crossed the line into adult territory today, whether she liked it or not.

"Say, do you know Kayla?" I asked.

"The blond werewolf chick?"

"Yes. I met her today over at Jolene and Alex's house."

Begonia pinched the skin on my arm. "You were over at the murder scene? Are you trying to make Sheriff Hugo hate you more?"

"I don't want him to hate me at all."

"Then stop trying so hard."

Sedgwick appeared above me. *He's waiting outside the coffee shop for you, Oh Merciful One.*

Keep it up and see how merciful I am, I said.

"I need to go, Begonia. We'll catch up later, okay?" I hurried over the cobblestones before she could stop me.

As promised, Daniel was waiting for me outside Brew-Ha-Ha. For a brief moment, I was able to observe him unnoticed. One look at his tall, muscular frame was enough to get my blood pumping. When he turned toward me and smiled, I nearly melted into the cobblestone.

"Your owl can be very aggressive," he said.

"Good afternoon to you, too," I said.

"Seriously, what do you feed him? Testosterone-laced mice?"

That sounded vile. "Sedgwick is what humans call an overachiever," I said apologetically. Actually, Sedgwick was what humans called a jackass, but I wasn't about to disparage my owl to the angel.

"So what's the emergency?" he asked.

I moved closer to him and lowered my voice. "Has Sheriff Hugo come to see you yet?"

His brow furrowed. "Sheriff Hugo? No, why?"

I took him by the elbow and guided him down a quiet alleyway. "Have you heard about Jolene?"

He blinked. "Jolene? No, what about her?"

I gave his arm a supportive squeeze. "She's dead, Daniel." It seemed incredible that I'd heard about Jolene and he hadn't. Then again, he was an expert at spending time off the beaten path.

His serene expression crumbled. "What happened to her?"

"No one knows. She was found on the kitchen floor by Kayla."

He nodded. "Her cousin." He blew out a breath. "Holy trumpets in heaven. Poor Kayla. And Alex…"

I mentally prepared for my next statement. "Kayla mentioned that you'd been coming around some mornings after Alex left for work. Is that true?"

"Kayla said…?" His hand covered his face. "Oh."

"I don't know how to interpret that, Daniel, and I'm damn sure the sheriff will take that tidy ball of incrimination and run with it. Anything to make his life easier."

His hand slid upward and combed through his blond hair. "I wasn't there today, Emma. I swear."

"That doesn't answer my question." Or maybe it did.

I could see he was struggling with his grief, so I gave him another minute to process the sad news. Unfortunately, I couldn't give him any longer than that because I knew Sheriff Hugo or his deputy, Astrid, would be hunting him down for questioning. They'd probably already been to his house by now.

"Daniel," I said. "I don't want to end up defending

you in court. Let's nip this in the bud now. Tell me everything so I can help you."

He grabbed my waist and pulled me toward him before attempting to launch us both into the air. Great balls of fire, I needed a warning before takeoff.

"Daniel, stop," I said.

"I won't drop you."

"That's not what I mean. Let's just sit in the coffee shop and talk. I'm sure we can find a quiet corner."

"But I need to think," he protested.

"Again?" He did more thinking than the statue of the thinking man and the statue had no other options.

"I need to figure out what to say."

I didn't like the way that sounded. "Daniel, please don't make statements that make you sound guilty."

He peered into my eyes. I stopped talking, momentarily dazzled by their turquoise hue. "Do you think I'm guilty?"

I snapped back to reality. "Of course not." I took his hand and dragged him inside Brew-Ha-Ha. "That's why I'm here to help you before this spirals out of control."

We were in luck. I spotted an empty table in the back corner of the room, right near the restrooms.

Under different circumstances, I would have preferred to sit as far from the restroom as possible, but we didn't have the luxury of choice.

"Would you like me to order something for us?" he asked.

"You stay here," I commanded, pointing to the secluded table. "I'll go and order. Try to keep a low profile." I didn't want the sheriff hunting him down before I had a chance to talk to him.

I placed my order and returned to the table, adjusting my chair so that I could block Daniel from the room's view. Not that it was easy to block a gorgeous, ridiculously tall angel.

"So describe your relationship with Jolene," I said. I cringed inwardly, not sure if I wanted to hear the answer.

"Strictly friends," he replied. The knot in my stomach unraveled slightly.

"Why were you visiting her in the mornings?" *Specifically, why were you waiting until her fiancé left the house?*

"We were offering each other support," he said. "She didn't want anyone in the pack to know."

Two mugs floated down in front of us, looking frothy and delicious. I'd ordered Daniel's latte with a shot of common sense. I wondered if he'd notice.

"Thank you," he said, and plucked the mug from the table for a greedy sip. "Gingerbread. This was a good choice."

I took a sip of my cinnamon latte with a shot of compassion. I figured if I was going to listen to Daniel's side of the story, I needed the boost.

"Support for what?" And why didn't she seek it from Alex?

He lowered his gaze. "Depression," he said softly.

"Jolene was depressed?" That wasn't a good sign for a woman about to walk down the aisle.

"She struggled with the town curse," he said. "She hated knowing she was trapped here with no way out."

A flicker of recognition sparked in my mind. When I first met Daniel, he was contemplating suicide on a cliff top. If I hadn't jumped out of my beloved green 1988 Volvo to save him, I wouldn't be trapped here now. Not that I blamed Daniel. To be fair, he saved me from getting crushed by my runaway car, which now lived at the bottom of Swan Lake.

"I see why she chose to confide in you," I said.

"We started talking last year. It was completely by chance. I was in the forest one night contemplating the state of the universe…"

I held up a hand. "You really have to stop saying things like that."

"But it's true."

What was the expression the other witches used? "Spell's bells," I said. "Okay, so you were Ralph Waldo Emerson-ing your way through nature…"

"Who?"

"Henry David Thoreau-ing?"

He shook his head. "I stumbled upon Jolene in a clearing. She was naked and crying."

Oh.

"What happened to her?"

Daniel looked thoughtful. "She was upset about the shifting ordinances and had decided to risk getting caught and go full werewolf. She chose an area away from town, not far from your house in fact."

"Did she hurt herself?"

"No, she'd shifted back to human because she felt guilty about breaking the rules. Then she was crying because she felt lost and alone. The wolf in her was desperate to roam. To leave Spellbound."

"But she couldn't."

"No, as you've learned."

I inhaled sharply. "So you talked."

"We did. And I shared my own feelings about the

curse and how it made me feel. It seemed to help to know she wasn't alone."

"She didn't think Alex would understand?"

He polished off his latte. A bit of foam stuck to his upper lip and I fought the urge to lick it off. *Down, girl.*

"You have to understand pack mentality. Werewolves are top of the food chain. They're all about power and strength. For them, depression is a sign of weakness. She was mated to a rising pack leader. She couldn't afford to drag Alex down."

"So you kept talking?"

"We began to meet regularly in the mornings after Alex left for work. We'd have coffee in her kitchen and help each other through the rough patches."

"Was Kayla there?"

"Not initially." He tapped his fingers on the table. "I can't remember exactly when she showed up. It was after a big fight with her parents. Anyway, it was good for Jolene, to focus on someone other than herself. It was only after Kayla came that Jolene started talking about having children. I viewed talk of the future as a positive."

"Did Kayla ever join your conversations?"

"Absolutely not. Jolene didn't want to burden

her." He dipped his head. "She seemed to be doing much better lately."

"When's the last time you saw her?"

He paused. "I think it was last week. She was ordering the flowers for her wedding in Petals. I passed by the window and saw her, so I went in to say hi."

"Was she alone?"

"No, her mother was with her. And Kayla and maybe Alex's sister. I'm not sure."

Witnesses were good. Of course, if most of their meetings had been in secret, it would be difficult to prove he hadn't been with her.

"Do you have an alibi for this morning?" I asked.

"No. I was alone."

The selfish part of me was relieved, but the practical part of me didn't like his answer.

"I think you should plop yourself in a chair in the sheriff's office and wait for him to show up," I said.

"But you don't trust the sheriff," he said.

"I don't, but what are your options?" The sheriff had proven himself lazy and would likely lunge at the easy option. He could easily paint Daniel and Jolene as star-crossed lovers. Desperate to keep his beloved from wedded bliss with another man, he murdered her. A paranormal Romeo and Juliet.

ANNABEL CHASE

"I could hide until this blows over," Daniel said.

"No, that makes you look guilty."

"They know I can't really go anywhere," he said with a shrug. "I'd have to emerge eventually. Hopefully, after they figure out the real reason for her death."

Instinctively, I reached for his hand. "Daniel, I don't want you to disappear."

He gave me a crooked smile. "Why? Miss me already?"

I finished my latte, letting the warmth thread its way through my system. "I don't want you to appear guilty to everyone in Spellbound. What if they stop pursuing the investigation because they're too busy pursuing you?" It happened all the time in the human world. The detectives became focused on one suspect and ignored all the other evidence.

He groaned. "You make a good point."

"So what are you going to do?" I asked.

"What do you recommend?"

I weighed the options. "How about this? Come and stay with me, that way I know where you are. If anyone asks, I can say that you're on a spiritual retreat or something and that I know where to find you in an emergency. And I'll do what I can to look into her death."

He leaned back in his chair. "A little soon to move into together, don't you think? We haven't even had our first date."

My stomach flipped like a pancake. Now was not the time for him to flirt with me. He'd just had a shot of common sense, for crying out loud.

"You're off the market, remember?" He told me he was turning over a new leaf, that he planned to redeem himself for past behavior and swear off the opposite sex.

He winked. "And you're far too sensible to get involved with a disgraced angel like me."

I sat up straighter. "That's right," I said with a little too much emphasis. Me doth protest too much.

He pushed back his chair and stood. "So let's go home, sweetheart."

I rolled my eyes. I hoped the investigation was wrapped up quickly. I had a feeling that between Gareth, Daniel and me, three was definitely going to be a crowd.

Sedgwick waited for us outside Brew-Ha-Ha.

Where did you find Daniel? I asked.

On a cliff top overlooking Swan Lake.

I should have known. His thinking spot.

He was reading a book of poetry, Sedgwick continued. *What's wrong with him?*

He's a delicate flower, I said. *And there's absolutely nothing wrong with that.*

Says you.

It was honestly one of the qualities I liked most about Daniel. Not the fact that he was broodier than a vampire, but the fact that he was willing to *feel*, even when it was difficult. Fallen or not, people could learn a thing or two from an angel like him.

CHAPTER 4

TOGETHER, we soared over the town, silent and serious. I clung to him for dear life and tried desperately not to lose my latte.

"Shall I carry you over the threshold?" Daniel asked, once we arrived at my house.

"Ha ha. Not remotely funny."

I unlocked the door and called out to Gareth. I wanted to give him an immediate update on the situation. He was going to love this arrangement. Any opportunity to torture me. He was quickly becoming the scary older brother I never wanted.

"Oh look," Daniel said. "There's Gareth's pet. With that patchwork head of his, he's really more of Frankenstein's cat, isn't he?"

Magpie trotted into the foyer, looking like the cat that ate the canary. For a brief second, I wondered if he had, in fact, eaten a canary. I fervently hoped none of my neighbors was missing a bird.

"If you're staying here, then you need to be nice to Magpie," I said. I didn't love the cat either, but this was his home and I wouldn't allow him to be insulted here.

"Oh, I see you've brought your fallen friend home," Gareth said, observing Daniel. "Be sure to put a sock on the doorknob. And not one of those unattractive knee socks you're so fond of."

"You put a sock in it," I said. "Daniel is staying here until a situation blows over."

"What situation?" He seemed intrigued. "Jealous husband?"

"Not your business."

"It's my business if he's staying in my house."

I gave Gareth my most threatening look. Granted, on a scale of Kansas to New Jersey, it was closer to South Carolina, but still.

"This is my house, remember?" I said. "When are you going to get that through your transparent mind?"

Daniel took a step backward. "Maybe this is a bad idea."

I spun around. "You. Stay put." I rounded on

Gareth. "And you. Stop being a curmudgeon. Daniel needs our help and we're going to offer it."

Gareth developed a sudden interest in the floorboards. "Fine," he muttered and then dissipated.

"There are several empty rooms upstairs," I said. "You even get a choice."

Daniel followed me upstairs to assess the bedroom options.

"Do you think maybe I should stay in the attic instead?" he queried. "What if someone sees me?"

"In one of the bedrooms?" I asked. "I don't see how that's possible. The only one here is Gareth and he can't communicate with anyone except me." I was such a lucky girl.

Daniel halted. "I don't want to create a problem for you. Sheriff Hugo already dislikes you. If he finds out about this…"

"Then it won't cost me anything I haven't already lost." I beckoned him forward. "Let's go, Wingman."

He chose the chintz bedroom, which made me laugh. Not that the alternatives were much better. Gareth had clearly opted to experiment when decorating the guest bedrooms. One bedroom was painted bright yellow and all the furniture was brass. Gareth referred to it as the sunroom. Although I'd tackled the downstairs, I'd yet to redecorate upstairs.

"Is there anything you want from your house?" I asked. "A favorite bedtime toy? Clothes? I'm happy to get it for you." I was asking to be nice, but also because I was nosy. I hadn't been to Daniel's house and was interested to get a peek inside.

He picked up a snow globe off the dresser and shook it. Fake snowflakes filled the glass, obscuring the snowman and reindeer from view. "No, thanks. It's a little dusty in here. Didn't you hire a fairy cleaning service?"

I snapped my fingers. Fiona owned The Magic Touch. She and her gang of scrubbing fairies would be a problem. I'd have to cancel their visits until Daniel left. "Old houses are dust magnets. I'll take care of it and make sure to cancel Fiona."

"Ask him if he likes his eggs scrambled or fried," Gareth said. "And maybe he'd like a mint on his pillow in the evenings."

I ignored him and focused on Daniel.

"I'm going to send Sedgwick with a note to Fiona and then I'm going to practice my wandwork for class. I'll make dinner in about an hour."

"Holy darkness, are you trying to murder him?" Gareth asked, clutching his chest.

"I'm a decent cook," Daniel said. "Why don't I make dinner for us?"

"Smarter than he looks," Gareth said.

"Do you like chess?" Daniel asked. "Maybe we could play after dinner?"

"That would be great." Except I had no clue how to play chess. "I'm planning an early night, though. I need to drop by the office in the morning before I go to class."

More importantly, I needed to restrict my time alone in the house with Daniel. It was hard enough to resist his charms in the great outdoors. In an intimate setting like this one, I'd be fighting an uphill battle.

He grinned at me, oblivious to my inner conflict. "This will be fun, spending quality time together."

My gut twisted as I forced a smile. "Can't wait."

"Nobody ever said angels were blessed with intelligence," Gareth said with a shrug.

Althea greeted me in the morning with my usual latte. I found it amazing that in such a short time I managed to even have a usual latte. As I took the cup from her hand, one of the snakes shot out from beneath her headscarf and hissed at me.

I jumped back, nearly spilling my drink.

"Down, girl," Althea said sharply. "You know

better than that." The snake recoiled and Althea gave me an apologetic smile. "Sorry, she wants to lick the foam."

Ugh. "Any appointments today?" I asked.

The Gorgon pretended to consult the papers on her desk, but I knew that was merely a formality. Work was slow thanks to a low crime rate and that was okay by me. Between classes and the new accusation against Daniel, I had enough on my plate.

"You have a client appointment in half an hour," she said. "A berserker named Linsey."

"What's the charge?"

"Vandalism. She already pled guilty."

"So what do I need to do if she pled guilty?" I hadn't made it to court in Spellbound yet, since my last client confessed to his crimes before the trial.

Althea looked thoughtful. "Why don't you ask Gareth what he would've done?"

I'd told Althea about Gareth's ghost. They'd worked together for many years and it seemed right that she should know. It was nice to complain to someone who knew him.

"That's a good idea," I said. "In the meantime, do you have any clue? If she'll be here in half an hour, I don't have time to run home." As far as we knew, Gareth was tethered to the house.

"From what I know, I think you should focus on reducing the sentence and minimizing any collateral consequences," Althea said.

"Collateral consequences?" I had no clue what that meant.

"Well, for example, Linsey is only eighteen. She's very young. Even though vandalism is a misdemeanor, it can impact her driver's license. Her current license can be suspended because she's under twenty-five. She could also lose her right to use magic."

Did berserkers use magic? The only berserker I'd met so far was Henrik, the barista in Brew-Ha-Ha. I hadn't bothered to research this particular brand of supernatural.

"What can you tell me about berserkers?" I asked.

"Historically, they were Norse warriors," Althea said. "They were known for being crazy and vicious on the battlefield."

Yikes. Good to know. "Does Linsey have any priors?"

Althea scanned the contents of a folder. "Yes, she was arrested for wearing animal skins to school just before graduation. She nearly wasn't allowed to graduate."

Wearing animal skins was against the law? "The charges were dropped?"

Althea nodded. "Just a slap on the wrist. If I remember correctly, they thought the stress of transitioning to the adult world was getting to her."

"Like you said, she's only eighteen," I said. "I would imagine eighteen is much younger here than in the human world. Are berserkers immortal?"

"No, but they have an extended lifespan."

"Could I please see the file?" If Linsey was going to be here in less than half an hour, I needed to study the details of her case and quickly.

Althea handed me the folder and I took it into my office. I sat down behind the desk and read the simple two-page document detailing her arrest. She had apparently vandalized the side of a jalopy with crude images. I looked to see whether there were any photographs in evidence. There was nothing in the folder. Maybe that wasn't standard procedure here.

I sipped my coffee and continued to read. The jalopy belonged to a twenty-year-old pixie by the name of Fern. I hadn't met her yet either. Fern work part-time at Trinkets, the gift shop. A knock at the door alerted me to Linsey's arrival.

She came alone. I expected her to arrive with parents. Where was her show of support?

"Hi, you must be Linsey," I said. She looked every bit the disgruntled teenager. Fire engine red hair that only a bottle or magic could provide--deep purple lipstick, and dark, heavy eyeliner. She wore a small gold hoop through her nostrils. Her fingers were covered in rings of varying metals. Naturally, she wore black from head to toe, including a pair of combat boots.

"You look young," she said, her upper lip curling slightly. "Are you the assistant or something?"

"Afraid not," I said. "I'm Emma Hart, your public defender. It's nice to meet you." I gestured for her to sit down. "I've just been looking through your file."

"Find anything good?" She was trying to give off an attitude, but I wasn't buying it. To be honest, she radiated pain and suffering. I wondered how much of it was fueled by angst and how much was fueled by actual trauma. If I asked the right questions, maybe I would find out.

"It says here you pled guilty to vandalism charges," I said. "Is that true?"

"Yep. Every word of it." She folded her arms, appearing to have no more to say on the subject.

"Do you know what the standard sentencing is

for a vandalism charge?" I asked. I wondered whether anyone had briefed her before she pled guilty.

"I don't know. A year?"

"That doesn't bother you? A year of your life?" I wasn't even sure if it was as little as a year, but I was still bothered by the fact that a year seemed to mean nothing to her. She wasn't a vampire. She wasn't immortal.

"I'm not exactly setting the world on fire," she said. "Maybe a year in the big house will be good for me."

I smelled Minotaur shit.

"Linsey, why don't you tell me exactly what happened in your own words?"

She raised a colorful eyebrow. "Why waste my breath? It's all right there in your file, isn't it?"

"I'm sure it is, but I'd like to hear the story from your own mouth." I clasped my hands together and put on a patient face.

Linsey shifted uneasily in her chair. "There's this pixie, Fern. Cute as a button. Everyone loves her." She rolled her eyes in disgust. "I couldn't take it anymore. I stole a can of fairy paint out of my neighbor's garage and went over to her house in the night.

I painted the side of her jalopy with amusing pictures."

"It says here in the file that you're a talented artist. Maybe you could funnel your artistic talents into something more productive."

"I don't think the artwork I drew on the side of Fern's jalopy is something the public wants to see." I saw the hint of a smile on her purple lips.

"Obscene, was it?"

"Very." She paused. "More anatomically correct than artistic."

"And all this because Fern is cute as a button?" I leaned back in my chair. "Sorry, I'm not buying it. What are you not telling me?" There was nothing in the file about motive. Not that they needed a motive for a charge like this. Still though, I wanted to know. To understand Linsey's actions.

"Why do you care?" She shifted to the side and placed her boots on the seat of the chair next to her. I said nothing. I figured she was just trying to get a rise out of me.

"She was a couple years ahead of me in school. A cheerleader. Always in student government. How is it possible to be someone that everyone likes?"

I shrugged. "I don't know, Linsey, but the reality

is, there are people like that in the world." Just like there were witches with a natural talent for flying on broomsticks. Not remotely fair, but c'est la vie. "They just radiate goodness and people respond to that. I think it's nice. Why does it bother you so much?"

Linsey glared at me. "No one is that nice."

"You think everyone harbors a dark side?"

"She fooled everyone except me with her cheerful smile and friendly attitude." She pressed her fingers into her cheeks, creating dimples.

"Who did she fool in particular?" Linsey was holding back. I could tell. "You clearly think she's fooled someone. Maybe someone you like or respect?" A light bulb went off in my head. Of course. This was about a guy. It was always about a guy.

Linsey's gaze shifted to the floor. "Doesn't matter," she mumbled.

"Of course it matters," I said. "Was there an incident? Is this a guy you like who likes her? It would be helpful to know."

"How could that possibly be helpful? Then he would know why I did it. That he was the reason." Her skin paled. "I don't want him to know. It's embarrassing."

"The vandalism is embarrassing?"

She exhaled loudly. "Not just the vandalism. The other stuff."

I skimmed the papers again. "What other stuff?"

She stared at me. "It doesn't say anything else?"

"Not in here. You need to tell me, though. If there's a chance it might come up in the courtroom, I need to know now."

Linsey nodded and moved her feet back to the floor. "I may have been a little out of my mind."

"Out of your mind? What does that mean? You were drunk?"

"I may have been sniffing a magic powder that night. And I may have turned up in her driveway wearing a wolf pelt."

"I guess the werewolves in town weren't too fond of that," I said.

"Especially because that was all I was wearing."

Oh.

"So when you sniffed this magical powder, did you know you intended to vandalize Fern's jalopy?"

"No. I was just upset. I had been downtown earlier and saw Fern on a date with him. It drove me nuts."

"So who's the guy?"

"His name is Tristan. He's a druid."

Another druid. "Is he related to Boyd, the healer?"

"His son," Linsey said. "He graduated with Fern. I'd always had a mad crush on him. I swore to myself that when I graduated school, I would get up the nerve to ask him out. I finally managed to convince myself it was a good idea, but when I tracked him down, he was out with *her*."

"I imagine after building it up in your mind after all that time, you found it quite difficult."

Linsey pretended to examine her blue fingernails. I was fairly certain she was trying not to cry. "It had to be her of all people. Miss Perfect. You've never seen a pixie this adorable."

In truth, I'd never seen a pixie at all. I'd take her word for it, though.

"Fern could have any guy in town. She's that kind of girl. Why did she have to set her sights on Tristan? He's so down-to-earth and funny." She laughed to herself. "He cracks jokes all the time."

"Linsey, you're going to live in Spellbound for a long time. Don't you think you could branch out a little? Find another male to be interested in?"

"I guess the only guys I'll be meeting now are prison guards." She tried to look unconcerned, but again, I wasn't convinced.

"Let me look into your case a little more." I glanced at the paperwork again. "Your court date is set for next week. Let's see if I can work my own brand of magic before then."

"You mean witchcraft?"

"No, lawyer magic." It sounded laughable even to my ears, but I was willing to try. Linsey was young and misguided. I didn't want the rest of her life ruined because of a crush on a druid.

"So that's it?" Linsey looked relieved.

"For today," I said. "I'll send an owl to schedule our next appointment. We'll definitely need to meet before your trial date."

"Okay," she said and paused. "You're not so bad."

"Save the high praise for when I've earned it," I said. "I do want to help you, Linsey. I just don't know if I can."

"At least you're honest about it," Linsey said and stomped her boots on the floor before standing. "That's more than I usually get from grown-ups."

As she left the office, her words echoed in my head. I was a grown-up.

I wasn't entirely sure how I felt about it.

CHAPTER 5

"ALTHEA, IS THAT YOU?" I called. I'd returned to the office after class to grab Linsey's file for a little bedtime reading.

I paused to listen. Usually the hissing from her head of snakes gave her away, but I heard nothing except the sounds of the town outside.

"Althea?"

The sinewy frame of Demetrius Hunt appeared in my office and I nearly fell off my chair.

"How did you do that?" I asked. "You're a vampire, not a ghost." A very hot, very sexy vampire.

"I'm sorry," he said. "I didn't mean to frighten you."

"It's okay," I said, my heart beating wildly. "It's just that Mumford attacked me in this office, so I'm still suffering from post-traumatic stress."

Mumford was the goblin I'd been assigned to defend when I first arrived in town. He'd been accused of stealing jewelry and I figured out in the nick of time that he'd also murdered Gareth to cover up his crime.

Demetrius smiled faintly. "I had to drop off paperwork at the registrar's office and thought I'd come by to see how you're getting on. I heard you're in the process of mastering the broomstick."

"Mastering is probably a bit of an exaggeration," I said, "but I did get through a few practice sessions. It helps that I'm allowed to ride tandem."

"I'm sure you'll get through it with flying colors." He smiled. "Literally."

"I wouldn't be too sure. I'm more of an earth-bound girl at heart."

"I wish I could help you," Demetrius said. "I'm afraid my bat form wouldn't be of much use to you, though."

"I appreciate the sentiment." It was for the best, really. Sedgwick would lunge at the chance to torment Demetrius in his bat form.

"I came by for another reason," Demetrius said. "Would you like to have dinner with me tonight?"

My mouth dropped open. "Oh." I'd only been out once with Demetrius, to the Horned Owl for drinks.

It had been a spur-of-the-moment thing and he'd given me a chaste kiss at the end of the night, if a kiss that sends shivers down your spine can be considered chaste.

He inched his way around my desk, closing the distance between us. "Do you already have plans?"

"No, no plans." Unless you counted the angel hiding in my house. Different type of plan.

I looked up at him, trying not to get lost in those deep, dark pools. His thick eyelashes alone were mesmerizing.

"Good. Then I'll pick you up at your house at eight."

My mouth became so dry that I couldn't force out a response, so I simply nodded.

"You'll like Serendipity," he added. "It's very elegant and the food is excellent."

Apparently, when a vampire says he's going to take you to the nicest restaurant in Spellbound, the correct response is not—"Oh, right. Serendipity. Daniel and I went there."

Demetrius stiffened. "Daniel Starr took you to Serendipity?"

"It wasn't a date," I said, quickly realizing my error. "We were going to buy new paint for the house and…" I trailed off. Every word out of my mouth made us sound like a couple.

"No matter," he said, his expression darkening. "Serendipity isn't the only place in town. Far from it."

"I don't mind going again," I said. "It was delicious."

"Absolutely not," he said, showing his fangs. "I have no interest in retreading another man's ground."

With comments like that, I half expected him to pee a circle around me. Or maybe that was more of a werewolf thing.

"We'll go to Moonshine," he said. "It's a personal favorite."

"Sounds great." I hadn't been to Moonshine yet, but I heard someone mention it in passing.

"I heard the sheriff wants to speak with Halo Boy in connection with a werewolf's death," Demetrius said. "Do you know anything about that?"

"Just what you heard," I said. "I don't see how anyone could think Daniel is involved. He'd never hurt anyone."

"He's hurt plenty of women in this town," Demetrius said.

"Okay, maybe emotionally," I said. "Not quite the same as murder."

Demetrius displayed his fangs again. It seemed to be the vampire equivalent of flexing his muscles. "I look forward to tonight."

He was so dramatic that I almost expected him to disappear in a puff of smoke. It was a bit of a letdown when he simply walked out the door.

I remained in the office after his banal departure, reading up on Spellbound vandalism statutes and sentencing guidelines. I needed to thank Gareth for keeping his office organized. His law books were neatly stacked on the bookshelves behind my desk. It made my life easier. I felt like I had so much to learn and precious little time to learn it.

"Where's Daniel?" I asked, bursting through the front door. I got distracted by Linsey's case and now had less than thirty minutes to get ready for my date.

Gareth appeared on the steps. "He flew to one of his thinking spots. He swore no one would see him."

"Does he just talk out loud and hope you hear him?" I asked.

Gareth shrugged. "Basically. He's very polite, I'll

give him that. And he seems to have taken a liking to Magpie."

That seemed highly unlikely.

"I need to get changed pronto," I said, and ran to my bedroom to ransack my closet.

"For what?"

"A date with Demetrius." I began pulling out hangers of clothes and tossing them aside. "He stopped by the office earlier to ask me."

"He's always been a persistent lad," Gareth said. "Definitely accustomed to getting his way."

"He's not getting his way with me, if that's what you mean," I said.

"I'm implying nothing of the sort." He drifted beside me and peered into the closet. "Wear that blue dress with the low neckline."

I stopped rifling through the clothes and glared at him. "I am not wearing a low neckline on a first date with a vampire."

He crossed his arms. "So you'd wear it on a date with a dwarf? That's discrimination."

"Go ahead and draft a petition about it," I said. "Anyway, I'm not going on a date with a dwarf." Not to mention dwarves seemed too short to appreciate the view. "You really can't cry discrimination just because I refuse to dress slutty for your friend."

"A low neckline isn't slutty," he said. "It's…accommodating."

"I would think wearing my hair in a bun would be accommodating for a vampire."

He rubbed his chin thoughtfully. "Now that you mention it…"

"I haven't told Demetrius about you," I said. "Do you want your friends to know?"

Gareth's expression softened. "I don't know. I suppose it would be nice."

"For some reason, they did seem to mourn your passing."

"For some reason?" he echoed, his hands flying to his hips. "I'll have you know I was a pillar of this community. I defended those who couldn't defend themselves. I…"

I began mimicking him with my hand. Very mature, I know.

He halted mid-sentence. "What are you doing?"

I hesitated. "Mocking you?"

"You are so lucky I'm a ghost," he said, wagging a finger at me.

I danced in front of him. "Go on. Bite me, or whatever it is you'd do in retaliation." I knew he couldn't. His form would blow right through me. One of the disadvantages to being dead.

"Did you used to behave like this with your siblings?" he asked, unimpressed.

I stopped dancing. "I don't have siblings."

"For for best, I think."

I pulled out a tasteful black dress and held it up.

Gareth scrunched his nose in response. "You'd look ready for a funeral."

"Fine." I placed it back in the closet. "I can't wear red because it's your color for grieving. I don't want to make him sad on our first date." I touched the fabric of a pretty green dress. "Maybe this one."

"Are you sure you want to go on this date?" Gareth asked.

"What do you mean?" I began to undress, then stopped. "Turn around."

He rolled his eyes. "You can't be serious."

"I don't want anyone watching me undress."

"Are you sure about that?" he asked. "I can think of a particular houseguest…"

I shushed him quickly. Daniel could return to the house at any moment.

"He can't hear me, remember?" Gareth said.

"Turn around," I ordered, ignoring him.

"Trust me, love. You'd show me nothing of interest."

"Is that what you told Alison?" As soon as the

words were out of my mouth, I regretted them. Alison was a siren and Gareth's former fiancée. Their relationship had ended the year before he died, and he'd never told her that he was gay. He'd never told anyone until me.

"Low blow," he said quietly.

"Sorry," I said. "I'm just nervous about the date." It was one thing to go to the pub with Demetrius for a few drinks. It felt very casual. Tonight seemed to have a more formal quality.

"At his core, Demetrius is a good guy," Gareth said. "But he may just be in it for the chase. To be the first to plant his flag in Emma's mound."

"Gareth!"

He gave me a sheepish grin. "That was rather crude, wasn't it?"

I remembered the hot vampire's negative reaction to Daniel's name. "I don't want to be a pawn in some macho game. How can I tell if he's genuinely interested?"

I stripped down to my underwear and pulled the green dress over my head.

Gareth took one look at me and smiled. "Oh, he'll be genuinely interested if you wear that. Demetrius is a neck man, but breasts run a close second."

"They're not too big, though," I said, cupping my boobs.

"Big, bigger, biggest. Does it really matter for a heterosexual male?" he queried.

Magpie rubbed against my leg before nipping the skin.

"Ouch," I cried. "Why does he do that?"

"It's a love bite," Gareth insisted.

"That is most definitely *not* a love bite." I scowled at Magpie and he hissed in response.

"He's the cat of a vampire, remember," Gareth said. "He's going to show affection differently."

"As in, not at all."

Gareth crouched down to speak to Magpie in a soothing tone.

"You spoil him," I said. "That's why he's such a beast to everyone else."

Gareth scowled at me and held his ghostly hands over the cat's misshapen ears. "Mind what you say. He can hear you."

I shook my head and retreated to the bathroom to freshen up. I wished I knew the spells to make myself look prettier. I stared at my reflection in the mirror as I ran a brush through my hair, trying to remember one of the improvement spells Begonia had done during class. I fetched my wand from the nightstand and quickly returned to the vanity.

"What are you doing?" Gareth asked.

"Privacy, Gareth," I said. "This is a bathroom."

"You're not on the loo," he said. "You're standing fully clothed in front of the mirror."

I closed my eyes in an effort to concentrate.

"You're not planning to do a spell on yourself, are you?" he asked.

I opened one eye and looked at him. "Why not?"

"Because you're sure to make a hash of it."

"Thanks for the vote of confidence."

"What are you intending to fix?" he asked. "Must be your hair. It is a wee bit frizzy."

My other eye flew open. "My hair is the one part of me I was going to leave alone."

"Oops."

"I'd like to do a makeup spell like the one Begonia used on me." I'd felt so confident and attractive after the last time. I desperately needed that feeling tonight.

"I'd advise against…" he began.

I turned to face him. "Out, Gareth. You're destroying my self-esteem."

"Youth today," he complained. "You all want to be

wrapped in cotton wool." He shrugged helplessly and glided out of the room.

I held up my wand and pointed it at my reflection. According to Lady Weatherby, the key to a successful spell was intent. I focused my will on myself and practiced an incantation in my head. I didn't want to mess it up.

"No!" I couldn't believe my eyes. "I wasn't finished."

I stared at my reflection in the mirror, gobsmacked. My boobs were a respectable size before, but now they were enormous. From grapefruits to honeydew melons. Had that been my true intent? Deep down, did I want bigger boobs? No, I really didn't. It was probably down to the conversation I'd had with Gareth moments before.

I dashed out of the bathroom, my ample cleavage on full display. "How did I manage this?" I caught sight of Gareth, pressing his lips together in a valiant effort not to laugh. "Don't you dare say 'I told you so.'"

"Wouldn't dream of it. How do you intend to correct this egregious error?" he asked.

"I have no idea," I said. "But I'll be sending Sedgwick to Begonia's with a plea for urgent help."

Gareth tilted his head, examining the state of my

chest. "If it's any consolation, you look amazing. I'm a little turned on and I don't even like boobs."

"I don't want him turned on," I said. "What if he bites me?"

"What if who bites you?"

Daniel's voice caused me to jump and my boobs bounced along with the rest of me. Oh no.

Daniel zeroed in on my chest. To be fair, it was hard to look anywhere else. "What in heaven…?"

"It was an accident," I said, awkwardly trying to cover myself. There was no good way to lay an arm across my chest without looking like I was groping myself. "I'm sending Sedgwick for help."

"If you'd had those in the lake, I wouldn't have needed to save you," Daniel said. "You could have used them as flotation devices."

Gareth howled with laughter. "He's funny. I never knew he was funny."

I glared at Gareth before focusing on Daniel. "No more boob jokes. I'm trying to build my confidence before my date and this is not helping." Not at all.

Daniel inclined his head. "You have a date?"

"Demetrius asked me to dinner," I said.

"Are you sure he didn't ask you to *be* dinner?" Daniel asked. "It's an important distinction."

"Hey," Gareth objected, but, of course, Daniel didn't hear him.

"You'll be okay on your own tonight," I said. "Just stay upstairs and don't answer the door."

Daniel raised a blond eyebrow. "All night?"

My cheeks grew flushed. "No, of course not. It's only dinner."

"He may want dessert when he sees you," Daniel said pointedly. "Two scoops, in fact."

Gareth pretended to fondle my boobs, but his hands kept gliding through me.

"Hello?" I said, waving at my pervert roommate. "Actual person here."

"Maybe you should change your dress," Daniel said.

"No," Gareth said sharply. "You look incredible."

I looked helplessly from one to the other. "I don't want him to be distracted. I feel like he won't hear anything I'm saying because he'll be focused on the twins."

The angel and the vampire remained silent and I realized they were both staring at my chest.

"Congratulations. You just proved my point!" I whipped around and ran back to the closet to find a more conservative dress.

Gareth followed me. Daniel was smart and maintained a safe distance.

"The navy blue dress with the cowl neckline," he said softly. "It will flatter your new figure and look elegant."

"It's not my new figure," I said, blinking back tears. "Is it?"

He made a gesture of trying to wipe a stray tear from my cheek. "Someone in the coven will be able to help. Just do your best to get through the evening."

"Do you think I should cancel?"

"Yes," came Daniel's reply from the hallway.

"Up to you." Gareth gave me a sympathetic smile. "But you do look hot...for a girl."

"Thanks, Gareth." I pulled the hanger from the closet and went into the bathroom to change dresses. "I take back what I said about you."

"What did you say?"

"Don't worry," I told him. "It was only in my head."

CHAPTER 6

THE WIND CHIMES signaled the arrival of Demetrius. He was a respectable five minutes late.

"You should consider putting wards around the house," Daniel said, as I left my bedroom.

"What are those?"

"Magical alarms. They can let you know when someone has stepped onto your property. You could also repel certain types of creatures. For example, if you didn't want vampires to come here, you could have a spell performed to keep them from crossing the property line."

"Like the town curse on a smaller scale," I said.

"The opposite really," he said. "It keeps them out rather than in."

"I don't think it's a coincidence that he chose vampires for his example," Gareth complained.

I ignored him. "I won't be late. Keep a low profile."

As I moved toward the stairs, Daniel's fingers lightly touched my arm. "You look very pretty tonight. I hope he appreciates it."

My heart seized. Why, oh why, did Daniel have to look at me like that? To talk to me like that? Why couldn't he simply slap me on the back and say, 'go get 'em, tiger?'

"Thank you," I mustered. I found myself fuming with each step I took. It wasn't my fault Daniel had chosen a path of celibacy and redemption.

I cooled down and released a soft sigh. Under the circumstances, my feelings were irrelevant. I wouldn't dream of getting between and angel and his halo.

I opened the front door and greeted my date. Unsurprisingly, his gaze went directly to my chest, but, to his credit, he immediately jerked his chin upward, as though aware of his faux pas.

"Good evening, Emma," he said. "You are a vision tonight."

"Thank you. You're not so bad yourself." He looked sexier than ever in snug dark denim and a short-sleeved, V-neck top that emphasized his arms and torso. He definitely knew how to show off the contours of his firm body.

"Demetrius always knew how to dress," Gareth said, echoing my thoughts.

"Goodnight, Magpie," I called sweetly.

"Faker," Gareth hissed.

"That's good of you to take care of that horrific creature," Demetrius said.

I resisted the urge to laugh as we left the house. I could feel Gareth steaming behind us.

"Is this your car?" I asked. The jalopy in the driveway was the closest thing to a sports car I'd seen in Spellbound. Sleek and black with shiny wheels, it was only roomy enough for two.

"It is. Do you like it?" He opened the passenger door for me and I swooned a little. As much as I considered myself a feminist, I couldn't deny that I liked people to do things for me and that included opening doors and pulling out chairs. To be honest, I didn't care if it was a man or a woman, as long as I didn't have to do it myself. I'd been taking care of myself for so long, I think I just liked the idea of someone else taking care of me for a change. Even in small doses.

With his car's supercharged magical engine, we arrived in town within minutes. Not much time for conversation. He left the keys with the elf valet and escorted me inside the restaurant, his arm slung around my waist. A possessive gesture or an affectionate one, I wasn't sure.

"Moonshine has live music," he said. "I thought you might enjoy the atmosphere."

He wasn't kidding. The moment we stepped inside, it was like walking into a huge party. The place had a New Orleans vibe—festive and fun with appealing food.

Patrons called out greetings to Demetrius. He was a regular, it seemed.

The hostess didn't bother to ask us how many in our party or if we had a reservation. She guided us straight to a cozy table smack dab in the middle of the busy dining area. I had no doubt it was because Demetrius liked to be on display.

"This place is fantastic," I said, trying to make myself heard over the live music. "The band is great." The music struck me as an interesting mix of rock and jazz.

"They're called Look Mom, No Wings," he said. "They play here a lot."

I checked out the members of the band. "I don't see any fairies."

"There's a brownie on sax, a satyr on drums, an elf on guitar, and an incubus is the lead singer."

Same as in the human world, groupies clustered in front of the small stage, singing along to the lyrics.

"Would you mind if I ordered for us?" he asked. "I have a few favorites I'd like you to try."

Normally, I wasn't adventurous with food, but since most food and drink in Spellbound were new to me, it didn't seem like a huge risk. "Sounds good." I surveyed the room for a server until I noticed Demetrius tapping spots on the menu. "What are you doing?"

"It's how we order here," he said. "I tap the items on the menu and the kitchen receives the order."

Wow. It was almost electronic—except magic.

Demetrius smoothed a napkin across his lap. "That's done. Now I have a fun question for you," he said. "If you could choose to be any species in Spell-bound, which one would it be?"

"You mean instead of a witch?"

He nodded.

"Okay, I'll bite." Inwardly, I winced. Did I seriously just say 'I'll bite' to a vampire? I needed my neck examined—my head! I needed my *head* examined.

"I think that's my line," he said with a gentle laugh.

My face was on fire. "I wouldn't mind being a siren. I always wanted to have a nice singing voice." Instead of the cat in heat sound I produced in the shower or the car.

"You just want to lure men to their doom," he said.

The food and drinks appeared on the table out of nowhere and my stomach rumbled. I didn't realize how hungry I was until now.

"Everything looks amazing," I said.

I managed one drink and half the food on my plate when I saw a familiar head bobbing through the crowd. Thank goodness.

"If you'll excuse me," I said. "I need the restroom."

"Of course." Demetrius smiled and those fangs glimmered in the candlelight. They were pointy teeth, for crying out loud. Why were they so attractive?

Begonia waited alone in the restroom. I locked the door behind me to be on the safe side.

"You got my message?" I asked.

Begonia's eyes popped at the sight of my enlarged chest. "Spell's bells, Emma. I got the memo, but I wasn't expecting them to be quite so big. You're almost pornographic."

She turned on the tap to drown out the sound of our voices.

"I'm not sure what I did wrong or how to reverse it," I said. "I hadn't even said the incantation when they burst onto the scene."

Begonia chewed her lip. "I don't think you did anything wrong."

"How can you say that? Look at me." I arched my back for emphasis, not that it was necessary.

"You can't reverse it," Begonia said, "but that's because you didn't do it."

I didn't understand. "Of course, I did. I was in the bathroom at home and…" My pulse began to race as the implications flashed through my mind. New clothes from Ready-to-Were suitable for a larger bust. I wouldn't be able to run anymore without falling forward. Okay, truth be told I only ran in an emergency, but I liked to know the option was on the table.

Begonia shook her head. "I swear it wasn't you, Emma. Whatever you did was a coincidence. This has Millie written all over it."

That made no sense. "Millie? Why would she…?"

Then it hit me. In class the day I turned Millie into a hairball, she swore revenge.

"Did she make a voodoo doll of me?" I asked. I was introduced to the remedial witches' voodoo dolls a few weeks ago. There was a secret underground lair where the younger witches congregated to spend time away from the rest of the coven. It was also equipped with the magical version of a television, for which I was eternally grateful.

"She must have," Begonia said. "She didn't share it with us, probably because she knew we'd stop her."

"So what do we do?" I asked. "Beg Millie to reverse the spell?"

"Or find the voodoo doll and reverse it ourselves."

"Should we go to the hideout?"

Begonia looked shocked. "You can't go now. You're on a date with Demetrius Hunt." She said his name with the reverence normally reserved for celebrities. I guess in Spellbound, the only celebrities were the residents.

"But this is more important," I said.

"At least wait until after the date," she said. "I'll meet you at your house. Send Sedgwick to let me know when you're on the way." She paused and gave me a sly look. "Unless you don't think you'll make it home tonight."

"Gak," I exclaimed. "Why does everyone say that? Yes, I am absolutely going home tonight." I didn't mention Daniel's temporary visit.

"If I were in your shoes"—She stopped and glanced at my chest—"and in your boobs, I would absolutely *not* be going home tonight."

"He is very sexy," I admitted. "But if he's immortal and we're both trapped here for our entire lives…" I trailed off. On one level, the curse made dating seem like such a bad idea. I quickly shook it off. I refused to adopt the mindset of the more cynical residents.

"So how's the date going?" Begonia asked. "Is he as dreamy as I think he is?"

"I'm having a good time."

When Begonia glanced away for a split second, I knew she had something else to tell me. "I hate to ruin your fun, but you should know that Sheriff Hugo has issued a code clover for Daniel," she said.

"What's a code clover?" It sounded too adorable to be problematic.

"If you see him, alert the sheriff or his deputy immediately."

Like an APB. Ugh.

"Is the sheriff telling people why?"

Begonia hesitated. "Because he considers Daniel to be a person of interest in Jolene's murder."

Not the news I wanted to hear, but not unexpected either. "Who told you that?"

"I was in Lady Weatherby's office when the owl arrived. He contacted all of the council members."

Great. Now everyone in town would be scouting for Daniel. I'd need to move quickly to help eliminate him as a suspect.

"This changes everything," I said. "I hate to say it, but now I'm definitely going to have to cut my date short."

"No, you can't." Begonia looked horrified. "What if he never asks again?"

"Then I guess he doesn't like me enough," I said. "Better to know now."

"Are you going to tell him why?" Begonia asked.

Good question. "I'm not sure. He and Daniel seem to have a weird competitive vibe."

"It's not weird at all." She held out her right hand. "Angel." She held out her left hand. "Vampire. They're natural frenemies."

"Wait for me out front," I said. "We'll head to the hideout first."

"Seriously? I thought you were eager to clear Daniel's name."

"I am, but I'm starting to get a backache." I stretched my back gently, careful not to pull a muscle. "I won't be able to do the legwork to help him if I can't walk tomorrow."

"Fair enough. How will we get there, though? I came here on foot."

"Broomstick?" I hated the idea of air travel, but I was willing to suffer if it meant getting this over with quickly.

"It's nighttime," Begonia said. "I'm not authorized to fly a broomstick after sunset yet."

More rules. "Okay, I'll figure something out. Meet me outside in five minutes." I sucked in a deep breath and checked myself in the mirror. "Wish me luck."

"Luck," Begonia said, and blew me a kiss.

I returned to the table, where Demetrius was chatting with the patrons at the table next to us. His gaze flickered back to me as I sat down.

"Everything good?" he asked, studying me. "You look unwell."

"What if I told you that we could keep the date going a little while longer, but that it involves a favor?" I quivered inside. Asking for favors made me uncomfortable at the best of times.

He leaned forward and looked into my eyes. "You need only ask."

A pleasant shiver ran down my spine. I didn't know what kind of vampire mojo was at work, but whatever it was, it *was* working.

"Can we cut dinner short and drive to another location?" I swallowed hard. "With my friend, Begonia."

A smile tugged at his lips. "You want me to accompany you and your girlfriend to an undisclosed location?"

That sounded much more risqué the way he said it. "I need to retrieve something," I explained, "but it's too far to go on foot and we're not licensed to fly after dark." Or at all, in my case.

"Sounds adventurous," he said with a wink and tossed his napkin onto the table. "Let's go."

He didn't seem the least bit bothered about skipping the rest of the meal.

"Thanks, Demetrius. I'm sorry to change the plan."

"No worries. I like when things get shaken up around here. Spellbound can send you into a trance if you're not careful."

That was a relief—not the part about the trance—but the fact that he was willing to roll with the punches. Definitely a tick in the 'pros' column. Not that I was making a mental list. Fine, I was making a list, but I'd never write them down. The only problem with the mental list was that Sedgwick had unfettered access to it. I really needed a spell that blocked Sedgwick from my private thoughts. I'd need to ask someone about that.

Demetrius paid the bill and escorted me outside, where Begonia was waiting patiently.

"Ah yes, your pretty friend," he said, flashing his fangs. Ever the show-off. "Hello again, Begonia."

Begonia turned pink. I wondered if that obvious blood flow was a turn on for a vampire. "Hi," she squeaked.

"Where's this second location?" he asked.

"I'll direct you," Begonia said, finding her voice. "Where's your car?"

At that moment, a valet pulled up with the black sports car.

"It only seats two," I said, remembering the sleek interior.

His dark eyes traveled over the pair of us. "You'll both fit if one of you sits on the other's lap." He seemed quite pleased with his suggestion.

"I'll sit on your lap," Begonia told me. "Your boobs will be like a springy cushion."

"And if all goes well," I said, "I'll sit on your lap on the way back."

Demetrius smiled. "And if all goes well for me, you'll both sit on my lap…"

"Nice try," I said, as the valet opened the passenger side door for us. Demetrius tipped him and slid into the driver's seat.

I settled into the car and Begonia squeezed on top of me. I hoped the roads were smooth or this was going to be more uncomfortable than I anticipated.

"Don't lean back so much," I said. "You're squishing me."

Demetrius had the decency not to laugh. "Where to, ladies?"

"You have to promise not to look," Begonia said.

"Sort of important when I'm the one driving," Demetrius pointed out.

Begonia bit her lip. "Right. Well, you have to promise not to pay attention to the route and to never return there."

"Vampire's honor." He held up his wrist and bit down with his fangs. Blood spurted and he sucked it away.

I gulped at the sight. Why couldn't he have been a

Boy Scout? I was pretty sure their honor code didn't involve blood.

Begonia nodded, satisfied. "Drive north. I'll tell you when to turn off the main road."

"You witches are bossy," he said with a sexy smirk. "I like it."

Who knew? A vampire with a submissive streak.

True to his word, Demetrius remained in the car while Begonia and I went to the secret lair. She placed her hands on the side of the hill and said the magic words to make the door appear.

The inside was spacious and inviting. I'd enjoyed several evenings here with the other girls, watching films from the human world and gorging on snacks from the Wish Market. It made me sad to think that Millie was so angry with me, she'd chosen to act out rather than talk it out with me. What I'd done to her was an accident. Everyone knew that. What she'd done to me was mean and deliberate.

"Should we check the basket?" I asked. The voodoo dolls were kept in a woven basket. I pulled out the one of Lady Weatherby with its little horned headdress. As tempting as it was to get back at her for tormenting me, I wasn't willing to mess with a witch of her stature.

"No," Begonia said. "Millie's too smart to keep it with the other dolls. We're in there too often."

I placed the Weatherby doll back in the basket and joined Begonia in the hunt for my likeness. We checked under cushions and in cupboards. We scoured the nooks and crannies but came up empty-handed.

"You don't think it's in her house, do you?" I asked.

"No way," Begonia said. "She'd be in serious trouble if anyone in her family found it. They would turn it over to the coven in a heartbeat. She wouldn't risk it. The doll has to be here."

"Her family likes to stick to the rules, huh?" I asked.

"They are overachievers. They're mortified that Millie is in the remedial program."

"But do they know she's the *star* of the remedial program?" I asked.

Begonia laughed. "She really is. No, they don't care. They just want her to pass all the tests so she can stop embarrassing them."

"That's awful." My grandparents would never have been embarrassed by my failures. They wanted to see me succeed, of course, but they knew I always gave my best effort and wouldn't choose to demoralize me.

I surveyed the room, trying to think of more places to search. A picture on the wall drew my gaze. It was a painting of a black cat on a rooftop stretching in front of a full moon.

"Is that picture crooked or is it just me?" I asked.

Begonia walked closer to inspect it. "Crooked." She removed it, revealing a small hole in the wall. "Jackpot." She reached inside and produced a voodoo doll with long, brown hair and, more noticeably, an obscenely large bust.

"What did she use to make those?" I asked, staring at the doll's chest.

Begonia peered under the doll's top. "Acorns."

"So do we just replace them with something smaller and do a spell?" I asked.

"Well, if you want your normal chest back, then we need to reverse it. Otherwise, you risk not getting your same boobs back." She stopped and looked at me. "Do you want your same boobs back?"

I nodded. Despite my moment of weakness in the bathroom, I knew they were Goldilocks boobs. Not too big, not too small. Just right.

"Thought I'd check first," Begonia said. "You

never know." She pulled out her wand and opened her mouth to speak.

"Begonia," I said, interrupting her. "Would you mind if I try to reverse it?" I thought of Lady Weatherby's insistence that I undo my own mistake. I created this mess. I should be the one to correct it.

Begonia handed the doll to me. "Whatever you want."

I retrieved my wand and pointed it at the doll. "Uncomplicate these friendship ties /make my chest its normal size."

Simultaneously, the acorns on the doll and my breasts began to shrink until they were back to normal.

"Yay," Begonia said, elated. "Great work, Emma. We need to tell Lady Weatherby. She'll be impressed."

"We can't," I said. "Not without getting Millie in trouble."

Begonia cast a sidelong glance at me. "You're not going to report her? You have the evidence in your hand."

I shook my head. "Millie lashed out because I embarrassed her. If what you say about her family is true—that she embarrasses them—then that's probably at the root of her behavior."

"You're more understanding than I am," Begonia said. "I'd be making another voodoo doll right now."

"That would get out of control really fast," I said. "Besides, I like Millie. I'd rather take the high road."

"Let's get back to Demetrius before he turns into a bat and leaves us here," Begonia said.

"We'd have his car," I pointed out.

She gave me a sheepish look. "Oh, right."

"What should I do with my doll?" I asked.

"Keep it as a souvenir," Begonia said.

With my luck, Magpie would turn the doll into his personal plaything. I didn't like the idea of him attacking me, even in doll form.

"No thanks," I said. "I think I'll just burn it." I hesitated. "I won't burn myself in the process, right?"

Begonia laughed. "No, silly. Not without a spell to accompany it."

I made a mental note. No spells while burning myself in effigy.

We returned to the car where Demetrius was gazing out the window at the stars. "It's such a clear night. Do the stars shine as brightly in the human world?"

"Same sky," I told him.

"What happened to your...attributes?" he asked, with a cursory glance at my chest.

I cleared my throat. "We performed a little magical surgery."

"Say no more," he said and started the engine.

Begonia sat down first and I plopped onto her lap.

"Thanks for the detour," I said. "Please drop Begonia off first, then you can take me home."

"I'd be happy to take you at home," he said with a smirk.

I fixed him with a hard stare. "You know perfectly well what I said. You have vampire hearing, remember?" I tapped the gear stick. "Now drive."

He revved the engine. "Bossy witches," he said, more to himself. "Damnation, I really do like it."

CHAPTER 7

IT WAS LATE when I returned to the house. Gentlemen that he was, Demetrius walked me to the front door. Under the shimmering light of the fey lantern, he kissed me for the second time. The first time had been after our evening at the Horned Owl. That kiss had been light, feathery, and completely unexpected. This one pumped blood to every outpost of my body.

"Thank you for an interesting evening," he said.

"In the human world, interesting isn't much of a compliment," I said.

"Make no mistake. In Spellbound, interesting is one of the highest compliments."

The sound of footsteps on the staircase inside caught his attention. "I think there's someone in your house," he said. A look of concern flashed across his handsome features.

"No, no. That's just Magpie," I insisted.

"I know I call that poor excuse for a cat a fantastic beast, but I don't think he weighs over two hundred pounds."

"You can guess someone's weight by the sound of their footsteps?" I asked.

He smiled. "Vampire hearing, remember?"

Note to self: tread softly around vampires.

"I am sorry about dinner," I said. "Next time I promise to finish the meal."

"Yes, next time I intend to make it to dessert," he said seductively.

My insides quivered. "Good night, Demetrius."

"Sleep well, Emma Hart."

He waited until I was safely inside before he returned to his car. I heard the roar of the magical engine as he pulled away.

I went straight upstairs to Daniel's room to see why he'd been lingering downstairs. He was under the covers, pretending to be asleep. I stomped over to the bed and ripped off the blanket. "I know you're awake," I said. "We heard you downstairs. I told you to stay out of sight. What were you thinking? Demetrius could have seen you."

He popped one eye open. "Did he ask before he kissed you? A true gentleman should ask first."

"That's none of your business," I said. "You know what is your business? Sheriff Hugo has issued a code clover for you."

"Good thing I'm here then," Daniel said. He sat up in bed, completely dressed.

"Do you need pajamas or any toiletries?" Like a toothbrush? I wondered if angels were susceptible to cavities and bad breath.

"I sleep in the nude," he said, and I nearly dissolved into the floorboards.

"Make sure you keep your bedroom door closed in that case," I said. "I don't need any midnight surprises."

He smirked. "So how was your date?" For a brief moment, I thought I detected a note of jealousy, but I knew that was just wishful thinking on my part.

"It wasn't what I expected," I said. And probably not what Demetrius expected either. "I don't know why you don't like him. He seems very nice." A little cocky, of course, but weren't they all?

"Of course he's very nice. That's how he lures you in."

"So you're angry because he's pulling a page from your playbook?"

He blinked. "What's a playbook?"

"Never mind." Football references would go over here like a lead broomstick.

"So are you going to see him again?" Daniel asked.

"I didn't come in here to reminisce about my date," I said heatedly. "I came to talk to you about Jolene. If the sheriff has identified you as a person of interest, we need to change his mind. Tomorrow, if possible."

"That's why I'm here, remember?" he said, spreading his arms wide. "What do you want to talk about?"

"I need leads," I said. "Can you think of anyone who might want to harm Jolene?" I hesitated, hating to speculate. "Given her experience with depression, is there a chance she may have taken her own life?"

He seemed momentarily stunned. "I suppose there is a chance." I knew what he was thinking. It was only weeks ago that Daniel had contemplated suicide. Under the circumstances, it was entirely reasonable to think that Jolene had done the same —successfully.

"We don't have results from the autopsy yet," I said. "That will help determine whether she killed herself." As far as I knew, there was no evidence of murder at the scene. No blood spatter. No sign of a weapon or forced entry. Suicide was a real possibility.

"I know someone who might be able to help," he said. "She's one of yours."

"A witch?"

He nodded. "Her name is Paisley. She works at Mix-n-Match."

Paisley. Yes, I met her when I went to buy the anti-anxiety potion. "What do I need to ask Paisley?"

"Jolene had mentioned to me that she was taking an anti-depression potion. She mentioned Paisley's name. Jolene had urged me to try it because she thought it was helping her." Not enough, apparently.

"And did you?" I asked.

He lowered his gaze. "No. I didn't want to use artificial means to drag myself out of the darkness. I wanted to do it on my own."

Typical male. "I know you're feeling a renewed sense of purpose now, but if you ever find yourself falling into another black hole, I hope you would consider it. I know in the human world, people manage to live fuller lives with the help of medication." Of course, it depended on the situation. I knew pills weren't the answer to every malady.

"You're my person, Emma," he said in earnest. "If

I ever find myself slipping into that black hole, as you call it, you'll be the first to know. I have a feeling if anyone can bring me back to the light, you can."

I blinked back tears. We'd only known each other for a short time. It seemed impossible that we could forge such a close connection. I felt it, though, and now I knew for certain that he felt it, too.

"I'm going to get a good night's sleep and so should you," I said. "I'll speak to Paisley tomorrow at the first opportunity. You stay here until I tell you it's safe to come out."

Daniel groaned. "Fine, but would you mind asking Gareth to stop stalking me? Even though I can't see him, I feel him hovering around me. Sometimes I feel like he's even mimicking me."

That sounded about right. "I'll speak to him."

"When you were in the human world," he said, "did you ever picture yourself sharing a house with a vampire ghost, a deformed cat, an aggressive owl, and a fallen angel?"

I couldn't help but smile. "Every day."

I headed over to Mix-n-Match during my lunch break. I hoped Paisley was working. I wasn't actually sure how many witches worked in the shop or what their schedules were.

Paisley was there when I arrived and she was alone. Bonus.

"Hey there, Emma," Paisley said. She seemed very nice the last time we met. Of course, everyone seemed nice compared with Jemima.

"Hi Paisley. How are you?"

"Business is slow today, but I expect it will pick up after lunch. How's the anti-anxiety potion working for you?"

"It's helping," I said. "I still feel anxious, but not to the point of panic. It seems to have taken the edge off."

Paisley smiled brightly. "Yes, that's what other people have reported as well. It doesn't cure it, but it makes it easier to cope."

"I don't mind being scared," I said. "That's a basic human emotion and I know, in some situations, the whole point is for self-preservation. But I need to be able to fly this broomstick. I don't want to be the only witch without a license."

Egads, I sounded like a pathetic high school student. The only one of her friends without a driver's license.

"I only wish it didn't taste so disgusting," I said.

"It would be much easier if I could just do an anti-anxiety spell with my wand."

"There are loads of spells you can do with a wand that are equivalent to a potion," Paisley said. "Unfortunately, anti-anxiety isn't one of them."

"That's okay," I said. "I'll survive." I hoped.

"So do you need something else?" Paisley asked. "Would you like to try a different potion? One that tastes better?"

I looked around the shop, just to make sure we were the only two present. "Actually, I want to ask you about the anti-depression potion that you sold to Jolene."

Paisley's expression shifted. Her smile disappeared and her eyes glittered with tears. "Such sad news," she said. "She was a ray of sunshine every time she came in here. Always so cheerful. It was hard to believe she was struggling with depression."

"I think she worked really hard to disguise it," I said. I knew that wasn't unusual for people who suffered from depression.

"When's the last time you saw Jolene?" I asked.

Paisley looked thoughtful. "Maybe two weeks ago? She'd come in for another bottle. She was close to finishing the one she had."

"And she seemed to think it was helping?" If it

was helping, then why would Jolene kill herself? I had to consider the possibility that the potion was like anti-depression drugs in the human world where the medication actually increased the risk of suicide.

"Sort of like you," Paisley said. "The potion hadn't eliminated the depression entirely, but it was helping her to cope. She was also trying other things."

"Other things?" I queried. "Like what? Did she say?"

"One of them is harp therapy," she said. "And I know because I recommended it. I go, too."

Harp therapy? "I've never heard of that."

"There are classes twice a week at the church," Paisley said. "I didn't join for the reasons Jolene did, but I find the music very relaxing. My home life is stressful at times, so it's a way for me to wind down."

"Who runs the class?" I didn't want to pander to stereotypes, but I wondered whether Daniel was involved. Somehow, I couldn't picture it.

"It's not Daniel, if that's what you're thinking," she said with a vague smile.

My cheeks colored. "No, no," I said quickly. Too quickly. "I thought maybe it was Myra, the church administrator." I'd met Myra when I was investigating Gareth's murder. She was a gnome, the nosiest gnome in all of Spellbound. She tried to get me to confess my sins, but I soon realized that she was more interested in collecting gossip.

"Myra lets us use the space," Paisley said. "But she's not involved in the program."

"When does the next class meet?"

"Tuesday evening," she said. "You're welcome to come. We're always happy to have new members."

I was definitely going to the next session. It would be the perfect opportunity to interview people about Jolene. If her death was a suicide, then the people she spent time with away from home might be the ones more likely to notice her state of mind. Her guard wouldn't be up as much with them as with Alex and the rest of her family.

"Paisley, could I have a sample of the anti-depression potion that she'd been using?"

"Sure. Let me get that for you." The minute she stepped behind the counter, Jemima swooped into the room. It was like a dark cloud settling above our heads.

"Good afternoon, Jemima," I said. I hoped she didn't ask why I was here.

"Haven't overcome your anxiety yet?" she asked snottily. "I heard you were flaunting yourself all over town with Demetrius Hunt last night. I guess *that* doesn't give you anxiety."

Great balls of nastiness. Jemima sure was a pill. I forced myself to be nice. She was a member of my future coven, after all.

"We had a nice time," I said. "Thanks for asking."

She squinted at me. "But I didn't ask…"

Paisley handed me the small sample. "Here you go. I hope it's helpful."

"Thanks a lot. And this is just between us, okay?" I didn't bother to nod toward Jemima, who was now busy applying a fresh coat of lipstick.

Paisley gave me a thumbs-up. "See you on Tuesday."

"I look forward to it."

Armed with new information, I made my way to the Pines to talk to Alex about his fiancée's depression. Although I wasn't surprised to see Kayla, I was surprised to see Jolene and Alex's families still there.

Alex greeted me like one of the pack. He hugged me and welcomed me into the house. "It's kind of you to stop by."

"I don't know that she's motivated by kindness,"

Kayla snapped. "I bet she's here because she likes the emo angel. She's probably here to defend him."

"Please forgive Kayla," Alex said with a reproachful look at the younger werewolf. "She's been irritable since Jolene's death."

"Even more than usual," a woman said from the living room. She was an older, more feminine version of Alex. She sat perched on the arm of a chair.

"Does your family come every day?" I asked softly.

"It's part of the grieving process," Alex explained. "When a werewolf dies, the extended family moves in and takes over the running of the household until the bereaved gets back on his feet."

Not unlike some human families. After my father died, my grandparents and other members of the Hart family seemed to be everywhere I turned. As a seven-year-old child, it was overwhelming. I felt like I had nowhere to hide and grieve in peace. Every room I entered, someone felt compelled to ask me how I was doing. How did they think I was doing? I was a seven-year-old orphan.

"I'm not here to defend Daniel," I said. "I'm here to ask you a few questions about Jolene. Is there somewhere we can talk in private?"

Now that I was standing in a room full of werewolves, my nerves were frazzled. What if they didn't like what I had to say? What would they do to me?

"Nothing's private in the pack," Alex said. "You can ask your questions here. If I don't know the answer, it's possible someone else here will. This is Jolene's mama, Patsy, and you met my folks before, LuAnn and Duke."

"Nice to see you all again," I said. I hadn't met his father, but it seemed rude to correct him. "I'm Emma Hart."

"She's the new witch," Kayla added.

Their eyes lit up in recognition.

LuAnn studied me from head to toe. "I heard you looked like a temptress." She turned to her husband. "She doesn't look like a temptress to me. Does she look like one to you, Duke?"

He checked me out as well. "No, Lu. Nothing like it. In fact, she's kind of homely. Not as bad as some of those witches, mind you, be she's hardly succubus material."

"Feel free to keep talking about me like I'm not here," I said.

Alex guided me to a quiet corner of the living room. "You know what? I think it's best if we talk over here." He lowered his voice. "You have to excuse my parents. They have a tendency to speak their minds and their minds aren't necessarily a pleasant place to glimpse."

"I know the type." I did. Back in the human world, I worked with a paralegal called Sheila, who was only too happy to tell you when you looked fat, or overtired, or point out when your socks didn't match. And she always found a way to do it when there was an audience. Needless to say, I didn't miss Sheila.

"What did you want to ask me about Jolene?" His expression was open and earnest. I felt a twinge of guilt for what I was about to suggest. We had to consider the possibility, though. It wasn't fair to pin a murder on Daniel if there wasn't a murder in the first place.

"Were you aware that Jolene suffered from depression?" I asked.

His gaze darted nervously over my shoulder to where the rest of the family lingered. "What do you know about it?"

"I know that she was taking a potion to cope with the depression. She was also attending a harp therapy class."

He narrowed his eyes. "What harp therapy class?"

"Twice a week. Tuesdays and Thursdays." I

produced the sample bottle of anti-depression potion from my handbag. "Have the sheriff check her system for this. I don't know if it's possible to overdose on it, but the lab experts will."

He stared at the small bottle for a beat before taking it. "How do you know all this?"

"Daniel told me."

At the mention of Daniel's name, his eyes suddenly glowed golden and I realized the wolf inside him was stirring. "Where is he?"

"I have no idea," I lied, "but he had nothing to do with Jolene's death. He was trying to help her."

"Help her how?"

"With her depression," I said. "They confided in each other."

I heard a low growl and realized it was coming from Duke, Alex's father.

"Nonsense. Jolene would never seek help from outside the pack," Duke said heatedly. "It's not our way."

"Maybe that's exactly why she felt she couldn't confide in one of you," I said. "Werewolves are supposed to be tough, right? Resilient?"

Heads bobbed up and down.

"Well, Jolene didn't feel that way about herself," I explained. "So she felt alone."

"She was getting married to the best wolf in the pack," Jolene's mother said. "She had nothing to be sad about, except maybe 'cause she didn't end up with the color wedding flowers she wanted on account of them being out of season."

It seemed depression was just as misunderstood in Spellbound as it was in the human world. "Depression like Jolene's isn't a simple case of sadness. It's not because she didn't get the wedding flowers she wanted. Or even for a more serious reason, like she didn't want to marry Alex."

"You need to stop talking right now, witch," LuAnn snarled at me. "No one here is interested in your drivel. Jolene loved my son and she couldn't wait to be the mama of his cubs."

"That's not what I'm saying." I didn't seem to be getting my point across. I was about to give up when I noticed a shadow pass over Alex's face.

"What is it, Alex?" I prompted.

His brown eyes met mine. "Emma's telling the truth."

LuAnn nearly fell off the arm of the chair. "What are you saying, son?"

Alex paced the length of the room, emanating pent-up energy. "It's all true. Jolene was real depressed. I told her to do whatever she had to do. I didn't know she'd been talking to Daniel about it, but it makes sense. Everybody knows he's a moody son of a bitch."

"You didn't offer to help her?" I asked. They were mated. It seemed like an obvious act of love and devotion. Your beloved is hurting—help her find a way to heal instead of leaving her to deal with it alone.

He kicked the wall hard, busting a shoe-shaped hole right through it. "What do I know about it? It just made me feel helpless." He faced me, his expression a mixture of anger and anguish. "We were getting married and all she could do was mope around the house feeling sorry for herself. How do I help her? It made me feel awful."

LuAnn stood and looked down her nose at me. "You've done enough here. I think you ought to leave."

With five angry werewolves staring me down, I was inclined to agree with her.

"I'll show myself out," I said, inching my way slowly toward the door. I didn't want to move too quickly and provoke the predators lurking within to give chase.

Once I closed the front door behind me, I exhaled the breath I didn't realize I'd been holding.

Although it was a long walk home, it gave me plenty of time to think.

CHAPTER 8

I RUSHED over to the field for another broomstick session. I'd gulped down my orange goo this morning, much to Sedgwick's amusement. I needed all the help I could get.

Professor Holmes used his wand to illustrate the course we'd take on our broomsticks for the final exam. A green light streamed from his wand to the blue sky above. A long-distance laser pointer.

"You must successfully complete four maneuvers in a solo run," he said. "The first one is a hard left." The green light bent sharply to the left. "The second one is a sudden, steep climb. You must fly twenty feet at a ninety-degree angle."

I gulped. A ninety-degree angle? Granted, I hadn't taken geometry in quite some time, but that didn't sound like a straight line.

"The third maneuver is the most complex." Professor Holmes pinned his gaze on Sophie. "Can you remind your classmates of this move?"

Sophie's jaw tensed. "The loop-de-loop."

"That is correct. You must circle up and over, executing a perfect loop."

I felt sick just picturing it. Upside down? I wasn't even sure why this maneuver was a requirement. It seemed more like a fun exercise for people who liked to fly on broomsticks. I was definitely not in that camp. I didn't even like amusement park rides that went upside down. I avoided roller coasters and anything involving heights. My grandparents weren't exactly begging to take me to an amusement park, so it wasn't an issue in my house.

"The final maneuver is, of course, the landing." His eyes wrinkled at the corners in that way that seemed to be the staple of older, distinguished men. "Easier said than done."

I raised my hand. "Professor? How do we know we've completed all four successfully?" I pictured a point system like in gymnastics. That was the only Olympic sport I'd ever watched.

"Believe me," he said. "You'll know."

Small comfort.

"Millie." He beckoned her forward. "Would you like to demonstrate the course?"

"Yes, Professor Holmes." Millie hopped on her broom and sped off without a backward glance. I had to hand it to her—she was a natural flyer. If we were on better terms, I'd ask her to practice with me.

Millie completed each move with grace and precision. She even made the loop-de-loop look fun. It was all well and good when someone else was on the broom, though. I knew I'd fall to pieces when it was my turn.

"I wrecked my landing last term," Laurel said in a low voice. "I think I took half the field with me."

"I don't think the grass has grown back yet," Sophie added.

"Sophie struggled with the loop-de-loop last term," Begonia whispered. "It's one of the tests she failed."

At least I wouldn't be alone then.

"Today we will practice all of these maneuvers," Professor Holmes said.

My stomach plummeted. *All* of them?

"Miss Hart, since the loop-de-loop is a complicated move, I've decided to pair you with Millie today."

Uh oh. It was unlikely he knew about the problem between Millie and me.

To her credit, Millie didn't complain. As long as she didn't push me off the broom when we were airborne, I'd be all right.

"Since the others have done this before," Professor Holmes said, "why don't you two start?"

My throat tightened.

"Sit in front of me," Millie directed. "Keep your hands on the stick at all times and, whatever you do, don't close your eyes."

Yes, yes. I knew not to close my eyes. I'd heard it enough times now that I'd started to repeat it in my sleep. Gareth initially thought I was trying to stay awake because he kept hearing me mutter, "Must keep my eyes open."

"I'm going to steer this time," Millie said. "You can do the next run."

The next run? My palms started to sweat. I wasn't sure the anti-anxiety potion was going to be potent enough for today's lesson.

We glided into the air and, once again, I marveled at Millie's prowess.

"You're so good at this," I told her.

She didn't respond. I took her silence to mean she was still angry with me.

"You're shaking, Emma," Millie said sharply. "Don't do that. You'll throw the broom off course."

"Sorry." That was like telling a leaf not to blow in the wind. Once my body began to tremble, it was very hard to stop.

"Emma, I'm serious," she said, struggling to regain control of the broomstick. "Vomiting is bad enough, but shaking is dangerous. It's a huge distraction."

I inhaled deeply through my nose and exhaled from my mouth. I'd taken yoga briefly in college and that was the only part I remembered. The rest was a jumble of pulled muscles and the inability to bend in unnatural ways. I also remembered a lot of giggling. Unsurprisingly, my attempt at yoga was fleeting.

We began the climb upward and I felt my body begin to tip backward. I clung to the broomstick, hugging it like my favorite stuffed animal from childhood. An owl called Huey. I'd refused to part with it, even to attend school. The therapist had told my father that the toy was a surrogate for my absent mother.

My beloved childhood toy was an owl. Why did I just remember that?

"Emma," Millie shouted, but it was too late.

I felt my body leave the broom and I hung in the

air, one hand gripping the handle. The broom began to spin out of control. The whole world turned and my stomach churned along with it. The last thing I remembered before slipping into darkness was throwing up and praying that I'd missed Millie.

I awoke in a familiar place. The healer's office.

"She's up," Boyd called, as he rushed to my side. "How are you feeling?"

"Dizzy," I said.

"That's to be expected." He gave me a sympathetic smile. "What happened up there? Millie said you couldn't stop shaking."

I told him about my anxiety and the potion I'd taken.

"It might be time to try a higher dosage," he suggested. "I can recommend a lotion as well, if you don't like the taste of the potion."

"What would a lotion do?" I asked.

"You rub it on your skin," he explained. "It basically acts the same as a potion, except your body absorbs it through the skin instead of digesting it."

Wow. I learned something new every day.

"Your friends are waiting in the reception area," he said. "Would you like to see them?"

"Is Millie okay?" I asked. I'd never forgive myself if I caused harm to anyone else.

"She's fine," Boyd reassured me. "She went home as soon as we told her you'd recover."

Millie went home, which meant she was not one of the friends waiting in the reception area. I tried to brush off the disappointment. What did I expect? I'd only given her one more reason to be upset with me.

A minute later, I saw the faces of Laurel, Sophie and Begonia peering down at me. I felt like a lab rat.

"Thank the stars, you're alive," Sophie said, and brushed the hair out of my face.

"You should have seen Professor Holmes," Laurel said, stifling a giggle. "I thought he was going to have a stroke right then and there."

"Is he here?" I asked.

"He was," Sophie said. "As soon as Boyd said you were out of the woods, he ran over to Lady Weatherby's office to report the incident."

Great. Just what I needed. More of Lady Weatherby's disapproval.

"Is Millie angry?" I asked.

"Who cares?" Begonia said. "It's not your fault."

"Well, it certainly wasn't hers," I said. "I couldn't stop shaking and then I couldn't focus. I remembered a toy I used to have. An owl. My mother had given it to me. That can't be a coincidence, right?"

"But your mother didn't know she was a witch," Sophie said.

"That's been my assumption," I said. "Maybe she knew after all. Or maybe she felt an affinity for owls but didn't know why. I guess I'll never know for sure."

"What was the owl's name?" Laurel asked.

"Huey," I said, smiling. "He was brown with yellow eyes." Not unlike Sedgwick, except Huey wasn't spotted.

"That's a nice memory," Begonia said. "I'm glad it came back to you, even if it was at an inopportune time." She bent over and hugged me.

Lady Weatherby entered the room, with Professor Holmes trailing behind her.

"You're alive, I see," Lady Weatherby said. She almost sounded disappointed.

"Surprise," I said weakly.

"Witches, please clear the room," she said. "You are dismissed for the rest of the day."

The other three girls exchanged surprised glances.

"Will Emma be able to go home today?" Laurel asked.

"Boyd says yes," Lady Weatherby said. "You can dote on your friend later. Right now, I need a word."

The trio left the room, leaving me alone with Lady Weatherby and Professor Holmes.

"You nearly killed yourself today," Lady Weatherby said. "As well as another student. What do you have to say for yourself?"

"I'm terribly sorry," I said. "I tried so hard not to be nervous, but my body refused to listen to my brain."

"Millie refuses to ride with you again and I don't blame her," Lady Weatherby said. "Being a part of the coven means being part of a group. One link in a long chain. You must put your own neuroses aside if you wish to join us."

"I didn't think I had a choice," I said.

Lady Weatherby glared at me. "You are in Spellbound now, Miss Hart, whether you like it or not. We have all made sacrifices here, some far greater than yours. Do not think for one second that you are alone in this."

She seemed to be taking my near-death experience very personally, as though I deliberately set out to die just to spite her.

"I'll apologize to Millie," I said. "I would never intentionally hurt anyone."

"Your intentions are irrelevant," Lady Weatherby said. "Do better or you may find yourself ex-communicated."

Tears stung my eyes. Ex-communicated? The coven would shun me?

"J.R.," Professor Holmes said softly. "Perhaps you're being too harsh on the girl. I was there, remember? She panicked. She's hardly the first witch to do so."

Lady Weatherby turned her attention to the elderly wizard and I saw him flinch. "If you have an issue with anything I've said," she said, "I would appreciate it if you spoke with me in private instead of undermining my authority."

Professor Holmes pressed his lips together. He was a sweet man and I appreciated his efforts on my behalf.

"Why don't we let the patient rest now?" Boyd suggested, coming into the small room. "I'll release her in another hour or so."

"As you wish," Lady Weatherby said. Without another word, she spun on her heel and left the room. Professor Holmes gave me a reassuring pat on the shoulder before following her.

Once they were out of earshot, Boyd came over to the bed, rubbing his hands together. "Now that

Little Lady Sunshine has left the building, who wants ice cream?"

"Are you feeling better?" Daniel asked.

I was at home, tucked safely in my bed, with a vampire ghost and an angel hovering beside me.

"Jittery, but otherwise okay," I said.

Daniel handed me a cup of tea on a saucer. "It's thistle and thyme."

"I had Magpie direct him to it," Gareth said quickly. "He doesn't know his herbs from his weeds."

"Thank you both," I said, taking a hesitant sip of the tea. The warmth shot straight to my belly.

Sedgwick flapped into the room. *The vampire is here.*

"Daniel, you need to stay hidden," I said. "Demetrius is here." I dragged myself out of bed and down the steps.

"What's he doing here?" the angel asked.

"He probably heard about the incident," I called over my shoulder. "You know how fast word travels in Spellbound." At the speed of light.

"Fix your hair," Gareth called.

There was no time to worry about my hair as I flung open the door. "What a surprise."

He seemed relieved to see me. "I wasn't certain you'd be able to answer the door."

"I'm sure the whole thing was blown out of proportion," I said.

He leaned against the doorjamb, the hint of a firm chest visible thanks to an open-collared shirt. "I heard you nearly fell to your death while on a broomstick with another remedial witch and freaked out the entire coven."

Okay, so maybe it wasn't blown out of proportion.

"Are you going to invite me in?" he asked.

I couldn't possibly let him in with Daniel hiding upstairs. Not with his vampire hearing.

"I appreciate you coming to check on me," I said, "but I actually need to get to work. I'm meeting with a client soon."

"Let me drive you then," he said. "You shouldn't be walking in your condition."

"My condition is fine," I assured him. I gulped the air, knowing I was about to say something I might come to regret. "Demetrius, you're a very nice—uh—vampire, and I've enjoyed spending time with you, but I think we should keep our relationship platonic."

His brow creased. "I'm confused."

"About which part?"

"The part where you don't want to jump my bones. That's never happened before."

I laughed. "No offense, Demetrius, but you're what? Hundreds of years old? Surely somewhere along the line, a woman decided not to sleep with you."

He scratched his chin thoughtfully. "No, I don't think so."

I shrugged helplessly. "It's not you. You're a catch, I promise. It's just that I'm still new here and I need to figure out my life before I get involved in a relationship."

He flashed his fangs in a last ditch effort to tempt me. I had to be honest, I wavered slightly. "Fair enough. You get settled in. There's plenty of time to get to know each other. In my experience, friends make the best lovers anyway."

Holy Vampire Hotness. I quickly pulled myself together. "Thanks. I knew you'd understand."

He winked at me. "I'm a patient vampire, Emma Hart. When you're ready to breach the friend zone, you know how to reach me." He turned around and sauntered down the porch steps, giving me a perfect view of his butt.

"You're drooling." Gareth's voice cut into my salacious thoughts.

I wiped my chin. "Am not."

"Nicely done, though. I like Dem, but I think you made the smart choice."

"Is he gone?" Daniel appeared at the top of the stairs.

"He's gone."

"What did he want?" he asked.

"To check on me."

Daniel crossed his arms. "He probably expected you to be unconscious and planned to drain your body of blood."

"You're ridiculous," I said. "Go back to your room."

"I can't," he said. "Magpie is on my bed and he's staring at me."

Gareth chuckled. "He is a naughty cat, isn't he?"

"I have to get to the office and meet Linsey," I said. "We need to prepare for trial."

"I wish I could go with you and offer assistance," Gareth said. "It's so boring floating around here all day."

"You should try," I said. "It would be helpful to have someone with knowledge advising me on the case."

"I assume you're talking to Gareth," Daniel said.

"Sorry, yes." I turned back to Gareth. "See if you can will yourself there. You have a deep connection to your office. There's no reason to think you can't materialize there. What do you have to lose?"

"You're going to leave me alone with the cat?" Daniel asked.

"Sedgwick is here," I said. "He'll protect you." A white lie. Sedgwick was no more fond of Daniel than he was of Demetrius.

Don't leave me here with the angel, Sedgwick protested. *He's so depressing.*

You're all a bunch of toddlers, I said. It would be a relief to flee to my office, even if it was to meet with a cranky teenager.

Don't blame me if you find feathers in your toothbrush, the owl said.

Why would I find feathers...? Never mind.

"See you later, Daniel," I called. They'd survive the rest of the day.

I hoped.

I lost Gareth as soon as we left our yard, but I carried on walking into town. I figured that if he didn't glide alongside me, he'd find some other way to materialize in the building.

By the time I reached my office, my feet were killing me. At this rate I would need another pair of shoes. I was already wearing out the soles of this pair.

Althea was watering a plant in my office when I entered.

"Any sign of Gareth?" I asked.

She shot me a quizzical look. "Is it possible for me to see any sign of Gareth?"

Good point. "Maybe a chilly breeze or a haunting sound?"

"None of the above."

I sat down at my desk to review Linsey's case again. It was always worth a closer look at the details.

"How about that?" Gareth popped into the office, looking around as though he'd never been here before. "I can't believe it. Somewhere else to go aside from the house. This is a dream come true."

"I'm not convinced that showing up at your musty old office is a dream come true," I said.

Althea jerked her chin toward me. "He's here?"

"To your left," I said. "Wearing the loudest outfit any ghost has a right to wear."

"Tell her she looks fantastic," Garth said. "Did she lose weight?"

"I am not asking her if she lost weight," I said.

Althea brightened. "I *have* lost weight. I cut back on the sugar plums and started on the elliptical. It's made a big difference."

"I told her so. Of course she would listen to me after I'm dead." Gareth rolled his eyes.

Althea stared at the empty space where Gareth actually stood. "He's complaining, isn't he? He wants to know why I only started listening to his advice after he died."

I chuckled. "You know him pretty well."

"Working in close quarters will do that to you." She gave me a sharp look. "You should remember that." She strode back to her adjoining office.

I wondered if Althea and I would end up working together for anywhere near as long she'd worked with Gareth. Time was a funny thing in Spellbound.

"So what time is our client due in?" Gareth asked.

"First of all, she is not our client. She is my client. You are merely here to advise."

Gareth folded his arms and floated above the chair. "Do you want my help or not?"

"Of course I do. But I want suggestions, not

mandates. Tell me about the potential judges. Talk to me about the prosecutor."

"The prosecutor is a wizard called Rochester. The judge will likely be one of three possibilities for a crime like this. There's Judge Hester Longbottom, a werepanther. Judge Lee Millville, a dwarf, and Judge Alayna Figueroa, an Amazon."

"Which one do I want it to be?"

He shrugged. "They all see sense. The wizard can get overly excited about pursuing tough sentences, so you need to watch out for that. He seems compelled to lock everybody away for a very long time. Sometimes I suspect he's in cahoots with the sheriff to wipe the town clean of any and all *potential* criminal activity."

"Wouldn't that be a good thing?" I asked.

"Not the way they do it," he replied.

"Noted," I said. "Are any of the judges tougher than others on sentencing minors?"

"Your client is eighteen," he said. "She's not a minor."

"I know. She's only eighteen, though. I feel like if a judge is lenient on minors, then he or she will be lenient on an eighteen-year-old. For this type of crime anyway."

Gareth seemed to consider it. "Judge Longbottom. She's the one you want in this case. She had a troubled son."

"What happened?" I asked.

Althea poked her head back in the doorway. "Are you talking about Judge Longbottom's son?"

"How did you know that?" I knew she couldn't hear Gareth.

"Everybody knows. It's a really sad story."

I looked to Gareth and he gestured toward his former assistant. "I'll let her tell it."

"Share with the class, Althea," I said. "Spare no details."

Althea came back into the room and took the chair beside Gareth. It was a shame she couldn't see him.

"There aren't a lot of werepanthers in town, you see," Althea said. "The other packs, like the werewolves, are much bigger. I think Evan felt left out a lot of the time. The packs can be very insular."

I noticed. The tension between the sheriff and Lorenzo Mancini over jurisdiction was probably the tip of the iceberg.

"Evan started hanging around with some of the less reputable characters in town. Supernaturals much older than him. He was impressionable."

"How old?" I asked.

"Seventeen," Althea said. "He left school at fifteen. He was an apprentice to one of the elves. A carpenter."

My eyebrows shot up. "An elf carpenter was a disreputable character?"

Althea shook her head sadly. "No, Mickey—that's the elf—tried to be a good role model for Evan. It just wasn't enough. Evan ended up stealing cash from Mickey's business over a period of months."

"What did he do with the money?" I asked.

"Illicit substances. Excessive time with a succubus. Activities your mother doesn't want to know about, especially if she's the town judge." Althea's mouth was set in a straight line.

"So how did he get caught?" I asked.

"It was his mother, actually," Althea said. "And she was the one who turned him in."

Ouch. That had to be tough.

"She spoke at his sentencing," Gareth interjected. "I was there."

"Were you defending Evan?" I asked.

"I was. And I consulted with Hester about the case in advance. She was determined that the court be hard on him. She wanted the maximum penalty. She figured by the time he got out that he would have learned his lesson."

"So is he still in prison?" I asked.

"Not anymore," Althea said. "He was killed on the inside. A fight with an inmate over stolen playing cards."

"I think Hester regretted her decision to be tough on him in hindsight," Gareth said. "I got the sense that she wishes she herself had been more lenient. That he needed something different than prison to change his path."

"Thanks for the information," I said. "Linsey's here. Gareth, be on your best behavior."

"Do I know any other kind?"

The door swung open and Linsey entered. Althea stood.

"Good afternoon, Linsey," Althea greeted her. "Can I get you anything to drink?"

"No, I'm good," Linsey said.

"No thank you," I corrected her. Holy crap, I wanted to slap myself. I sounded like my grandmother.

Althea returned to her own office and closed the adjoining door.

Linsey looked the same as the last time I'd seen her, except today her hair was shocking blue, like one of those troll dolls I used to collect. Even the texture looked similar. I wondered how she managed to do that.

"So have you found a loophole yet?" Linsey asked. Attitude was rolling off of her in waves. She didn't seem as relaxed as the first time we met.

"Everything okay, Linsey?"

She glared at me. "I'm about to go on trial. How can everything be okay?"

I tapped my fingers on the desk. "What happened? Did you have a fight with someone? I'm getting a very aggressive vibe from you right now."

She seemed taken aback that I would call her out on her behavior. "I did, actually. My parents."

"What happened?" I asked. "Did you ask them to come to this appointment?"

She nodded and sniffed. "I went by the house to ask them if they'd come. They wouldn't even speak to me. My father stood on the other side of a locked door and wouldn't open it. Like I'm some kind of violent criminal. What's wrong with them?"

"Your parents are berserkers, right?"

"No. I'm adopted. My biological parents died when I was young."

That hit close to home. "How old were you?"

"Five. They went hiking together in the mountains and that was it."

"That was it? Did they die of exposure?"

Linsey plucked an imaginary thread on the chair. "No, it was a murder-suicide. My dad killed my mom and then himself."

Her revelation nearly knocked me out of my seat. "Where were you?" She obviously had no close relatives if an unrelated couple had adopted her.

"I was with them," she said.

My heart stopped. "You were there?"

"I didn't see anything. I mean, I saw their dead bodies, but I didn't see him do it. He made sure that I was out of the way before he went psycho."

"You were in the mountains," I said. "How did you survive?"

"When I realized they were dead, I retraced our trail. I met up with a dwarf about halfway back to town. He brought me to the sheriff. I was adopted by my parents not long after."

Normally that would be a good thing, but in Linsey's case, it didn't seem to have panned out.

"I'm so sorry, Linsey," I said. "What a traumatic experience for you."

"The worst part is," she said, "I've always felt like my adoptive parents were a little bit afraid of me. That what my father did might somehow rub off on me. We're berserkers. We're known to go crazy. But

I behaved all through adolescence. I never gave them a moment's trouble until last year."

"What happened last year? I saw in your file that there was an incident before graduation."

"I was starting to have problems with my parents. They didn't like my hair or my makeup. Every little thing I did, they seem to take as a sign that I was going to go crazy. It almost became a self-fulfilling prophecy."

"What kind of species are your adoptive parents?"

"They're leprechauns. They couldn't have children and they desperately wanted a little girl. Then I became available. This little blond girl in braids. I think the taller I grew, the more intimidated they became."

"They're leprechauns," I said. "It's not hard to be taller than them."

Linsey chuckled. "True. I just think they let their fears get the worst of them. And then, of course, I started acting out because they expected me to act out. It's been a vicious cycle."

"I hate to tell you this, Linsey," I said. "But you're not telling me anything new. What you're describing is very normal in families with a teenager. True, your circumstances suck. I still think you have a chance to turn things around, though. You don't have to let your past dictate your future."

Linsey smiled at me, a genuine smile. I felt a rush of warmth spread through my body. Maybe I'd gotten through to her.

"She trusts you," Gareth said. "That's good."

I was so wrapped up in my conversation with Linsey, I'd forgotten he was there.

"I heard you almost died on a broomstick," Linsey said. "You must be the crappiest witch ever."

And, that quickly, the teenager was back.

CHAPTER 9

I MOVED BRISKLY around the kitchen, trying to fix myself something quick for dinner. Takeout allowed me to be a lazy cook in the human world, and magic allowed me to be a lazy cook here as well. Not that I was complaining.

Gareth watched me from the sidelines, endlessly amused. "Did you not learn how to do anything useful in the human world?"

I wrestled with the pot of sauce, trying to keep it from bubbling over. "I took care of myself," I shot back. "Just because I don't know how to use all of these magical kitcheny things doesn't mean I'm incapable."

He laughed. "Magical kitcheny things? You're holding a pot."

"If you're going to stand here and mock me, then do it somewhere else."

"That doesn't make any sense," he said.

I tried not to trip over Magpie as I shifted back to the cutting board. It was wonderful not to have to chop vegetables myself. Lucy, my fairy friend, had explained enchanted knives to me, so I picked one up at the Wish Market. I watched now as it diced my vegetables into neat little squares.

"Do you know anything about covens?" I asked.

"I'm a vampire. What makes you think I know anything about covens?"

"Well, presumably you were a vampire before you got trapped in Spellbound. Did you ever have encounters with witches outside of this town?"

"Aye, back in the old country. Witches were different then. A lot scarier."

"Because they were more powerful?"

"No," he said. "Because they were so ugly." He shuddered. "It was frightening to behold them."

I threw a dish towel at him, but it passed right through him and fell to the floor. "You're horribly sexist."

He chuckled to himself. "It's so easy to get a rise out of you. I wonder if this will ever get dull."

"So tell me about the covens in the old country. How are they different other than being uglier?"

"They were much more into rituals, for one thing. And far more secretive."

"That's probably just the result of the witches here being trapped in the town," I said. "They don't have the luxury of being secretive." Not in a town with a gossip chain as potent as Spellbound's.

"I don't pretend to know everything about the coven here," Gareth said. "But I know far more than I knew about any of the other covens I encountered outside this place."

"Did you ever meet anyone like me? A witch with an owl as a familiar? Or one that could see ghosts?"

"If I had, I wouldn't have known it. I wasn't a ghost then, was I? And we had plenty of owls. Hard to say whether any were psychically linked to the witches." He gave me an apologetic look. "I'm sorry, Emma. I do wish I could help you more. I think it's important to know about one's origin."

"I never felt that way before," I said. "But I have to say, it's been weighing on me ever since I arrived. Now that I know I'm a witch, I'd like to know everything."

"What's stopping you?" he asked. "You have access to books, to the library."

"Well, I *am* busy."

"Not the right kind of busy," he said with a wink.

"Gareth, there will come a day when you regret wanting me to be the right kind of busy. We live together, remember? What will be seen cannot be unseen."

His expression softened. "It's a big house," he said. "I always thought there was plenty of room for more."

"Don't you dare start talking to me about babies," I said. I scooped the vegetables into a bowl and returned to the stovetop where the pan was heating up over a magical blue flame. I dumped the vegetables into the pan and listened to them sizzle.

"Bear in mind, love, that I must now live vicariously through you. As depressing as that is."

"If you could touch things, then you could help me research." I had to figure out a way for Gareth to interact with solid objects. At least it would give him something to do. "Who in town knows anything about ghosts? I know I'm the only witch who can see you, but surely there must be some other kind of psychic in this town."

Gareth looked thoughtful. "Aye," he said. "You're right. We should try Maeve McCullen."

My brow lifted. "The banshee?"

Gareth nodded. "I don't know why I didn't think of her before. Banshees have a connection to death. She must be able to see apparitions."

"Perfect. Where can I find her?"

"At the playhouse most days. She practically lives there. She loves the stage and the limelight." He seemed heartened at the thought of seeing her again. "I was always rather fond of Maeve."

"Do you think you can materialize in the playhouse?" I asked. "Or should we invite Maeve here?"

"I'm happy to see where else I can go," he said. "I assumed I would only be able to appear in places I had a strong connection to, like my office or maybe the country club. I haven't tried random places in town that I've been."

"Did you attend her shows?"

"Frequently," he said. "I have a deep affection for the dramatic."

"No kidding," I replied. I stirred the sauce in with the vegetables. It was starting to look like an actual meal. Go me!

Gareth wrinkled his nose in disgust. "You're not going to eat that are you?"

"Way to harsh my mellow, Gareth."

"I don't even think Magpie would eat that."

"Sometimes I think it would be better if you were

seen and not heard. Maybe there's a way to turn down the volume on you." I'd have to ask Maeve.

"Try it and you'll regret it," Gareth warned. "This is likely how hauntings get started. A disagreement between the living and the dead undead."

"Keep up the attitude and I'll start burning sage," I countered. "See how you like that."

He gave me an approving nod. "I'll say this much for you, Emma Hart. You're tougher than you look."

When I came downstairs wearing a white cotton dress, Gareth burst into laughter.

"Where are you going dressed like that?" he asked.

"Harp therapy," I said, and glanced down at my dress. "What's the problem?"

"There's no requirement that you look pure as the driven snow in order to pluck a few strings."

"White seemed appropriate." I wanted to blend in as much as possible. It was hard being the new witch in town.

"I guarantee I know most of the girls in harp therapy," he said. "Trust me. Not one of them should be wearing white."

Paisley waited for me in the driveway and we

drove in her jalopy to the church. It felt good to give my feet a rest.

The church was just as pretty as I remembered from my first visit. The building was Romanesque, made of gray stone with rounded arches and one large tower. The angels carved from stone, however, were nowhere near as handsome as Daniel.

"There's a room downstairs where we play," Paisley said.

I followed her through the beautiful church with its stained glass windows, careful to avoid Myra, the church administrator. I'd met the gnome when I first moved to town and found her to be a little odd and a lot nosy. I didn't need her to see me attending a harp therapy session. She seemed to trade in gossip.

Downstairs was a room with three rows of chairs and multiple harps. The instruments were much bigger than I expected.

"Harps are available to rent or purchase," an elderly man said. "But not today. Consider today your taster session."

"Emma Hart, meet Ramon Ramirez." Paisley smiled at the older gentleman. "He's the best folk harp player in all of Spellbound."

"I offer private lessons too," he said, and wiggled his eyebrows. Oh my.

"Thank you, but let's see how the taster session goes," I said.

"I think you'll find it relaxing," Ramon said. "Music is food for the soul."

"And I'm sure it's been a stressful time for you," Paisley said. "Harp music will certainly lift your spirits."

"I hope so," I said. "I heard it helped Jolene a lot." I watched him for a reaction.

Ramon shook his head sadly. "Poor Jolene. That girl had her whole life ahead of her. Such a waste."

"You think she took her own life?" I asked, sitting down beside him.

"No," Paisley said. "Of course he doesn't."

Ramon glanced quickly at Paisley. "You don't?"

"I think the harp music had a positive effect on her," Paisley said. "She always seemed to leave here in a good mood."

"Didn't mean it lasted," Ramon said. "Maybe the demons came the moment she returned home and closed the door on the world. Nobody except Jolene knows for certain and she sure isn't telling."

"That's not necessarily true," I said. "If she was murdered, then there is someone else who knows."

Ramon flicked a dismissive finger in my direction. "Just because you arrived on the heels of a murder doesn't make every death in town a homicide. There are a lot of residents here and they're not all immortal." He began to pluck the strings of his harp. Even his casual plucking had a beautiful, haunting quality to it.

"Cookies," someone cried and the attendees leaped from their seats to swarm the table.

"You haven't tasted cookies until you've had Lorna's chocolate and sunshine treats," Ramon said, moving more quickly than I expected a man of his age to move.

"Chocolate and sunshine?" I queried.

"You'd better grab one now," Paisley urged. "They won't last. I swear her cookies are half the reason anyone shows up."

At the table, I was greeted by a wall of bodies, reaching and grabbing the cookies on the plates. I stood on my tiptoes and tried to peer over the heads of the crowd.

"Use your magic," someone whispered.

I glanced down to see a dwarf beside me. "You can't get through either, huh?"

He shook his head. "Most weeks I end up scooping up the crumbs just to get a taste."

That didn't sound hygienic. "I'll see what I can do." As discreetly as possible, I removed my wand from my waistband and pointed it in the general direction of the cookies. What kind of spell made sense in this situation?

"Jolene was be able to squeeze right through," the dwarf continued. "I think the others were afraid she'd bite them."

"Jolene wasn't aggressive, though, was she?" I asked.

"Oh no. Never," he said. "It's just that most of us in this group are of the dwarf and elf variety. If a werewolf wants in, we're gonna move. And fast."

"Did you like her?" I asked.

"Everyone liked Jolene," he said. "Even those of us who were intimidated by her. She was a real sweetheart."

I wished her ghost would show up like Gareth's did. Maybe if I waited long enough, I'd find her and get the answers we were looking for. Unfortunately, if she didn't kill herself, we couldn't afford to wait. The killer could strike again or disappear before being brought to justice. Even though the inhabitants were trapped within the town boundaries, there were plenty of places to hide...for a long time, if necessary.

"The cookies," the dwarf said, his tone urgent.

I kept my wand steady. "No need for a fuss/more

cookies for us." For a brief moment, I thought it was a bust. Until the cookies began flying off the plates and smashing into people.

Uh oh.

The attendees who were there for a relaxing evening of harp therapy ran screaming as cookies became missiles. Heads ducked and bodies dropped to the floor to avoid being smashed in the face with a chocolate and sunshine cookie.

The dwarf remained standing, grinning broadly as he caught any cookie within reach and shoved it into his mouth. "This is the best class ever," he said. His words were nearly unintelligible thanks to the amount of cookie stuffed inside his chubby cheeks.

From her position on the floor, Paisley tugged on my pant leg. "You need to reverse the spell."

I dropped down beside her. "I don't know how. Can you do it?"

Paisley produced her wand and the incantation tumbled from her lips. Cookies fell to the floor, smashing to pieces.

I cringed. "Do you know any cleanup spells?"

Paisley sighed and twirled her wand in a tiny circle. The cookies reformed and flew back to the plates on the table.

"I'm not eating them now," someone said. "They were on the floor."

"More for me," the dwarf said, and scooped up a handful. The rest of the attendees returned to their chairs.

Paisley gave me a disappointed look. "I'm going to have to report this."

"To Lady Weatherby?" I asked, praying the answer was no.

"I'm sorry. I don't want to, but the rules are clear. If someone tells them what happened and I failed to report it, I'll be in trouble too."

"What will happen?" I asked.

"You're still new," Paisley said. "I'm sure they'll go easy on you."

If Lady Weatherby had her way, I doubted they'd go easy on me. She seemed to want to make life as difficult for me as possible, which seemed unfair given that I didn't ask for any of this. I was perfectly happy back in Lemon Grove, Pennsylvania. True, I didn't have any family and friends were few and far between, but I'd been content.

"Miss Hart," Ramon called. "Come and play. I think you could do with a little harp therapy."

Once again, I took the empty seat beside him and studied the large instrument in front of me.

"Observe," Ramon said, and I watched his fingers manipulate the strings. The sound was mesmerizing and, after a while, I felt ready for sleep. It didn't get more relaxing than that.

"You try it," Ramon urged.

I touched the strings.

"They won't bite you," he said. "It's a harp not a vampire."

I plucked one string, then another. No matter what I did, the resulting sound was melodic. "Is this magic?"

"No," Ramon said with a smile. "It's just a harp."

Once I started, it was hard to stop. I kept trying to make the next tune more appealing than the last. It was exhilarating. When the announcement came that class was over, I felt a wave of disappointment wash over me.

"I think I need a harp," I whispered to Paisley. I wondered if Daniel knew how pleasant harps were. I'd need to enlighten him.

"It's good, isn't it?" she said.

"I wish it had been enough to save Jolene," Ramon added.

I think everyone agreed on that score.

CHAPTER 10

"THERE YOU ARE," Daniel said. "Come with me."

I was bent over Magpie's bowl, spooning in a can of tuna. "Huh?" Without my latte, I wasn't completely awake yet.

"What do the humans say?" he asked. "Time to get back on the unicorn?"

"Back in the saddle," I corrected him. "We don't have unicorns, remember?" I paused. "Why am I getting back on a unicorn?"

"The broomstick," he said. "You need to practice."

The color drained from my face. "No, no. I've resigned myself to failing this class. There's no rush, right? I mean, I'm stuck here for the rest of my life."

"Emma Hart," he said firmly. "You can't let fear win. You're better than that."

"I'm really not," I said. "Besides, I have class with

159

Lady Weatherby today. I need to keep my courage intact."

He held out his hand. "What good are these wings if I can't use them to help a friend in need?"

I stroked the soft, white feathers. "They make excellent dusters."

He glowered at me. "Outside. Now."

"I haven't taken my anti-anxiety potion today," I objected. "I'll vomit on you."

"No, you won't," he said. "You'll vomit on the trees in the forest. They're hundreds of years old. They'll survive."

"For the love of disco, go with him," Gareth urged. "Make the bloke feel useful. I'm tired of him moping about the place."

I shifted my gaze from Gareth back to Daniel. Did he have to look so earnest?

"Okay," I relented. "Let's go while it's still daylight."

We walked toward the forest behind the house until we reached a small clearing.

"We'll start here," he said.

"Start what?"

"You're going to ride me like I'm your broom," he said.

Heat rushed to my cheeks. "What? I can't do that."

"Of course you can. Just climb on my back and clasp your hands around my neck. Or my waist. Whatever's more comfortable."

"Won't I make it difficult for your wings if I'm on your back?" I asked. A lame protest, but I had to try.

"Plenty of room," he said, flapping his large wings. "If you wrap your legs around me here"—he patted his hips—"you'll be well clear of the wings."

The hottest angel in the world just told me to wrap my legs around him. My whole body was about to burst into flames. Well, on the plus side, spontaneous combustion would save me from broomstick class.

Daniel turned his back on me and crouched lower so that I could climb aboard. "Now or never, Emma."

"Never?"

He glanced over his shoulder and grinned. "I won't let you fall, you know that."

I did. I trusted him. For whatever reason, I'd trusted him from the moment I met him.

I pressed against the length of him, wrapping my arms around his neck and praying I didn't accidentally choke him to death.

"Legs," he prompted.

I hopped up and gripped his waist with my thighs. The thick feathers created a soft, fluffy saddle.

"I'm going to shoot straight into the air," he warned me. "Then I'm going to fly upside down, just like your loop-de-loop. Your job is to keep your eyes open and don't let go."

My mouth went dry. "Okay, I'm ready," I choked out.

He shot into the air like Superman and I clung to him, struggling to quash the queasy feeling in my stomach.

"Flying is a gift," he called into the wind. "You have to learn to embrace it."

I'd rather just embrace Daniel. "Warn me when you're going to do the loop."

He didn't warn me. We went up and over and, miraculously, I managed to keep hold of him. It probably helped that I had no interest in letting go of him, in the air or on the ground.

"Are you still with me?" he asked.

The breeze tickled my nose as we sailed through the air. "Still here."

"You did well, Emma. How about another loop?"

I winced. "One more and that's it."

We completed one more loop as promised and I steered him to the ground, narrowly avoiding the tops of the oak trees on the edge of the forest.

Daniel landed on his feet and I reluctantly slid off his back. A chill ran through me as I separated from him.

"How was that?" he asked.

"Not so bad," I admitted, thankful that I retained the contents of my stomach. "But that's because you're an expert flyer."

"Confidence can take time," he said. "You'll get there. I know you will."

"Thanks, Daniel. I appreciate your faith in me."

He grinned. "And I appreciate your faith in me."

I surveyed our landing site. "So what now?"

"Why don't we take a walk in the woods?" he proposed. "It's good for the soul."

A scenic stroll through the forest sounded ideal. Something to calm my frayed nerves and give Daniel a break from hiding in the house.

"Lead on," I said.

Daniel threaded his way through the tall trees and I hurried to keep pace beside him.

"This is almost as peaceful as harp therapy," I said.

"Wait. You went to harp therapy?" Daniel asked. "I didn't know that."

"I went to get information about Jolene," I said. "She apparently started attending to see if it alleviated her depression. I'm surprised she didn't mention it to you."

"You really liked it?" He sounded skeptical.

"When I can afford it, I'm going to buy one."

He whistled. "That's an endorsement if I ever heard one."

"Maybe that's what's missing for you," I said. "Harps and bugles." Or was it trumpets?

Daniel chuckled. "I doubt the missing piece in my life is a musical instrument." He stopped and examined a few leaves. "These are poisonous. Try to avoid skin contact and definitely don't ingest them."

"I don't plan on feasting on leaves anytime soon," I said.

"You never know," he said. "If you get lost in the woods and need food or water, you might be tempted by the wrong things."

"Oh, I'm always tempted by the wrong things," I said, and slapped my hand over my mouth. I did not want Daniel to know about my conflicting feelings for him.

"Are you talking about Demetrius?" he asked.

Inwardly, I breathed a sigh of relief. "I just meant in general. I told Demetrius that dating him wasn't a good idea."

His brow lifted. "You did?"

I nodded. "That's what I told him when he came by the house. I'm new here. I need to figure out my life. If my first move is to get involved with the town's most notorious vampire playboy...I think I need to get settled before I introduce a romantic element into my life."

"Sounds reasonable," he said. "Did you have anyone special back in Lemon Grove?"

"No," I said. "I worked a lot and didn't really make time for a personal life." Probably because I was afraid of having one. If I had people I cared about, then I risked losing them. In my experience, the negatives far outweighed the positives.

"Don't do that here," he said. "This is your chance to start over. To create the life you always wanted."

I resisted the urge to look at him. Part of me wanted to confess my feelings for him. I knew one glance at his angelic face would do me in.

A lump formed in my throat. "I won't. The coven wouldn't let me anyway. Lady Weatherby seems determined to break me."

"She probably wants you to catch up to the rest

of the witches in your class," he said. "She must think you have potential or she wouldn't bother." He plucked a few flowers from an obliging bush and handed them to me. "Wildflowers to brighten your kitchen."

I accepted the makeshift bouquet and inhaled their fragrance. "Divine," I said. Like you.

"More importantly, not poisonous."

"I'll make a note of it."

We walked in companionable silence, listening to the birds and the scurrying of tiny feet. It was so easy to spend time with him.

"Are we going somewhere in particular?" I asked.

"Do we need a destination? Sometimes it's nice just to wander."

"Why do I get the feeling it's not your first time?" I stopped to admire a misshapen tree. "Wow. This is the coolest tree I've ever seen." It rose almost thirty feet off the ground, stark white with branches that beckoned us. It managed to be both creepy, yet strikingly beautiful.

He followed my gaze. "It's looked like that for as long as I can remember."

"Really?" I found that curious. "Shouldn't trees grow and die here?"

"They do. Plants and flowers grow." He gestured

to the flowers still in my hand. "That tree is a land-mark, though. It's ancient."

I pressed my palms against the sturdy trunk. "Not the least bit hollow either."

Daniel's eyes sparkled. "Speaking of hollow, I have something to show you." He walked around the base of the tree and squeezed between two over-grown bushes. "This used to be a path, but it seems Mother Nature has reclaimed it."

I followed him between the bushes, trying to avoid getting scratched by the brambles. After fighting my way through the thicket, we emptied into a small clearing where we were confronted by a massive tree. It had to be at least seventy feet tall. The base of the tree was hollowed out, and I noticed what appeared to be wooden slats on the inside of the tree.

"Is that some kind of ladder?" I asked.

"It is." He eyed me carefully. "I know you're not a fan of heights, but I think you'd appreciate this."

I ducked inside the hollowed portion of the tree and began to climb. I left the bouquet on the ground, took a deep breath, and followed him up the ladder.

"Who built this?" I asked on the way up. Conver-sation would keep me from remembering I was gaining altitude.

Daniel glanced down at me. "No one knows. I don't think many residents even know it's here."

When we arrived at the top, I realized that it was much more than a lookout post. It was, in fact, an elaborate tree house with a huge platform that offered an unobstructed view of the skyline.

"Let me guess. It was one of your thinking spots." I bit back a smile.

"A long time ago," he said. "I haven't been here in ages."

Someone else clearly had. There was an empty bottle on the platform. "What is that?"

Daniel picked up the bottle. "Scorpion's Tail."

I stared at the bottle. "Poison?"

"Hardly. It's basically lemon fizz mixed with some type of strong alcohol."

"Oh. Like a wine cooler."

"What's a wine cooler?" he asked.

"The go-to alcoholic beverage for every girl in high school where I grew up. They didn't like the taste of beer, but they still wanted to be cool and drink."

He set down the bottle and faced the skyline. "It's so peaceful up here. I don't know why I stopped coming."

I joined him as close to the edge of the platform as I dared to get. "It is very pretty. And quiet."

"It's not far from your house," he said. "Maybe this can be your thinking spot."

"I'm not Winnie the Pooh."

Daniel shot me a quizzical look. "Who?"

"You don't know Winnie the Pooh?"

He wrinkled his nose. "Whatever it is, it sounds disgusting."

I laughed. "I actually think he's right up your alley. When I eventually make it over to the library, I'll see if any of his books are there."

"I'll go with you," he said. "I haven't been to the library in a long time."

"What do you do all day other than fly around and mope?" I asked. "Have you ever considered starting a business?"

He sat down on the edge of the platform, his legs dangling over the side. "I've thought about it."

"And?" I remained rooted to the middle of the platform. Daniel had the benefit of wings if he slipped off the edge. I had no such escape hatch.

"I couldn't decide on the type of business."

"You must have a lot of interests," I said. "Couldn't you choose one to focus on? A philanthropy even?"

"I'll give it some thought," he said.

"In your thinking place?"

"Naturally." He tipped his head back and smiled at me. "I like that you're willing to mock me."

"Because you like the abuse?"

"I don't know," he replied. "I feel like it shows a level of trust. That you know I won't take it to heart."

Unlike Daniel, the professional thinker, I'd never given it much thought. "I guess that means Gareth and I trust each other too." Because mockery seemed to be the basis of our relationship.

"You have to, don't you? You're permanent roommates now."

I rolled my eyes. "Yes, we'll be like an old, married couple in no time. All barbed comments and no sex."

"To be fair, you wouldn't be having sex with him even in solid form."

Gareth had given his blessing for me to tell anyone and everyone about his sexual revelation. He seemed to enjoy the range of responses.

"Do you think Jolene ever came up here?" I asked. Between harp therapy and potions, she seemed to be searching high and low for some sense of tranquility.

"If she did, it wasn't with me," he replied. A deep

sigh followed. "I really respected her, Emma. She worked so hard to overcome her depression and now this." He paused. "She deserved a better outcome."

I inched closer to him, still painfully aware of the seventy-foot drop. I was worried that my body would go into full-blown panic mode. I wanted to comfort him without the sudden need for him to comfort me.

I got close enough to place a warm hand on his shoulder. "By all accounts, she'd fallen in love with Alex and was looking forward to her wedding. She'd found hobbies to lift her spirits. Whatever happened to her, you were a positive force in her life. Remember that."

His fingers brushed my own. "Thanks, Emma." He peered up at me. "How would you feel about flying down?"

My hands flew to my hips. "I say all these nice, comforting things to you and that's how you plan to repay me?"

"What if I throw you off the platform and then swoop down and catch you?" he suggested. "That might be fun."

"Fun?" My eyes bulged and I backed away from the edge. "Are you trying to give me a heart attack?"

He began to laugh and I knew I'd been had. "You really make life worth living. You know that?"

CHAPTER 11

WE ARRIVED at the academy classroom to find a note pinned to the door with instructions to meet Lady Weatherby at a place called the Labyrinth.

"This is so exciting," Sophie said.

"I'm not really in the market for excitement right now," I replied.

Laurel clapped her hands together. "The Labyrinth is going to be so much fun."

The words 'fun' and 'Lady Weatherby' didn't go together in my mind. Something else was afoot.

"Maybe it's a reward for our hard work this term," Begonia said.

"Or punishment for our mistakes," Millie said with a sharp look in my direction. I briefly wondered if Paisley had reported the cookie incident from harp therapy.

"Only one way to find out," I said. "Let's go."

The whole setup reminded me of an elaborate bounce house for children. Of course, whatever Lady Weatherby had planned for us, I had a feeling it was not child friendly.

"Markos has kindly offered to allow us the use of his facilities," Lady Weatherby said. "He is a good friend of the coven."

I raised my hand. "Excuse me, Lady Weatherby? What exactly will we be doing in the bouncy castle?"

"All in good time, Miss Hart," Lady Weatherby said. "The five of you will be divided into two teams. The teams need to find their way out of their respective mazes."

"Don't you think I should be a little bit more experienced before you throw obstacles in my way?" I asked.

"Like the way you threw cookies in everyone else's way?" Lady Weatherby asked. The other witches looked at me blankly. "You needn't worry, Miss Hart. We've opted to overlook your most recent indiscretion."

I blew out a breath and tried to relax.

"The terrain inside is soft and springy," Millie said. "She probably thinks you're less likely to get hurt this way."

There had to be more to this game than simply finding the exit.

"What's the prize?" Millie asked.

Lady Weatherby chuckled deeply. "Must there be a prize? Can we not win for the sake of winning? I will never understand the younger generation."

"Is it just the first team member to get out of the maze?" Sophie asked. "Or does the whole team have to be out to win?"

"Good question for a change, Sophie. All team members must be out of the maze." Lady Weatherby stood by the entrance. "This is not your typical maze, witches. The terrain was designed by Spellbound's premier architect. No one builds a maze like a minotaur."

Translation: expect the unexpected.

"Do we get to choose our teammates?" Millie asked.

"I pulled names from the coven hat this morning," Lady Weatherby said.

I didn't really mind who was on my team. I figured no matter what, I was the weak link. If this had been playground dodgeball, I would've been chosen last.

"Laurel, Begonia, and Sophie. Stand to the left, please. Millie and Emma, stand to the right."

"It's not fair," Millie said. "It's basically three against one."

I winced. So now I didn't even count.

Lady Weatherby narrowed her eyes at Millie. "I think you will find there are two witches on your team."

"I'm at a disadvantage," Millie insisted. The disadvantage, of course, being me.

Lady Weatherby's steely gaze fixed on Millie. "You're smart enough for two, wouldn't you say?"

Millie straightened. "Yes, Lady Weatherby."

"Are we allowed to use our wands?" I asked.

"You will use anything at your disposal," Lady Weatherby said.

"Is there a time element?" Millie asked.

"No time element. When I say 'begin,' you will enter the maze." Lady Weatherby held her wand in the air and fired it like a pistol. I jumped at the sound. "Begin."

Begonia's blue eyes were round with fear. Of the three of them, I knew Laurel would be able to keep a clear head.

I turned to Millie. "The sooner we start, the sooner we finish."

"It's a bounce house designed for children," she scoffed. "How bad could it be?"

We started down our assigned path. The inflatable walls were too high to see over or around. We could still hear the chatter of our friends on the other side of the wall.

"It's soft material," I said. "Watch." I threw my body against the wall and bounced off, landing hard on my butt.

Millie rolled her eyes. "Please tell me you meant to do that."

"Anything to ease the tension," I said weakly. I stood up and brushed off my bottom. "But the terrain is designed to be soft. Lady Weatherby doesn't want us to get hurt. She just wants us to be inventive." True or not, I needed to boost my confidence. At least I'd taken my anti-anxiety potion this morning. That would help me not to panic.

We walked further until the sounds of the other witches died away. After a few more steps, the interior opened up and we came upon a rope dangling from an invisible ceiling above. Below was a pool of water.

"Water?" I breathed. "Is she nuts?" Witches couldn't swim. In fact, my mother died from drowning. I wondered if the other witches were encountering a pool of water, too.

Millie tugged on the rope. "I guess we're meant to

swing across to that ledge." She pointed to the inflatable ledge on the other side of the pool. I estimated it to be about fifteen feet away.

"Is there magic we can use to get ourselves across?" I asked. Too bad we didn't bring a broom. I would choose a low-flying broom over water any day of the week.

"Be quiet and let me think," Millie snapped. She closed her eyes, mentally running through any potential spells.

"I don't think I can swing across without falling in," I said. My upper body strength was nonexistent. Add to that my fear of water and we were looking at a disaster. "Can you think of a spell that involves swinging over long distances?"

Millie shushed me and covered her face with her hands. "Emma, I am trying to figure this out."

"Sorry," I mumbled. I could feel the panic rising inside me. I was pretty sure Millie felt the same way. She was no more likely to survive the water than I was.

"If only it were cold enough to be ice," I said. "Then we could skate across."

Millie peered at me through her fingers. "What did you say?"

"Nothing. Just wishful thinking." And I didn't

even like the cold. I much preferred Spellbound's temperate climate.

"Emma, that's it," she said excitedly. "I know a spell that can freeze water."

"Seriously?" That was music to my ears.

"My sister taught it to me last year when we wanted to prank my brother."

"You froze a pool for a prank?"

She huffed. "Obviously not. We froze his bath water just as he was getting in. He slipped and fell. Grabbed the shower curtain on the way down and took that with him. It was hilarious."

It didn't sound hilarious. Then again, I wasn't a fan of comedy pratfalls.

"I bet the rope is a diversion," Millie said. "It's here to make us think we need to use it."

That Lady Weatherby was tricky. "Would you like to do the honors?"

Millie took out her wand, focused her will, and pointed at the pool. "As gentle as a morning breeze/make this pool of water freeze."

We watched in anticipation as the water slowly formed an enormous solid cube. As Millie stepped forward, I stopped her with a hand. "Give it one more minute. Be sure it's frozen all the way through." The last thing we wanted was to fall in. Then we risked hypothermia as well as drowning.

We used the rope to ease down onto the surface of the pool. It was cold and very solid. Holding hands, we carefully made our way across. It was almost enjoyable.

"I've never been ice-skating," I said. "Have you?"

Millie shook her head. "Witches tend to avoid any activity involving water, even if it's frozen."

"Lady Weatherby must've been very confident that we'd figure this out. Otherwise, I'm surprised that our first obstacle would be so dangerous."

We made it to the other side and I boosted Millie so that she could climb up to the ledge. Once she was safely there, I saw a flash of hesitation in her eyes before she leaned over to help me. Would she really have left me here?

"One obstacle down," I said cheerfully. "Who knows how many left?" It was not a comforting thought.

"I wonder how the other girls are doing," Millie said. "I worry about Laurel. She's so young."

"Laurel's the last witch I'd worry about," I said. "She's very capable for someone her age." It was true. Laurel was going to make an excellent witch someday. With Sophie and Begonia there to help, they would be fine.

The next obstacle we encountered was a wall. There seemed to be no way around it. That meant we would have to go over it. I couldn't see how to gain a foothold. The material was smooth and there was no obvious way to gain purchase.

Millie stared upward. "How high do you think this goes?" she asked.

"No clue," I said. "Is there a spell for leaping tall stories in a single bound?" A Superman spell, perhaps.

Millie scratched her head thoughtfully. "I can't understand why Lady Weatherby felt it was fair to just have the two of us on a team. I have to do all the thinking."

"Hey," I protested. "I may not know the spells, but it was my idea to turn the pool into ice."

Millie had the decency to blush. "I would've come up with that answer eventually, though."

A little credit would have been nice, but my priority was getting out of here.

"I remember a spell that Ginger taught us," Millie said. "No, wait. That involved a potion, not a wand."

"Doesn't matter," I said. "Lots of spells with potions seem to have a wand-based counterpart.

When I went to Mix-n-Match, Paisley mentioned that there were lots of spells that you could do with the wand that were equivalent to a potion."

Millie's eyes lit up. "You're right. The potion we made with Ginger was a bubble spell. We rose in the air and floated around the exercise room." She smiled to herself. "That was a good day."

I whipped out my wand. "Okay. I'll try this one." I inhaled deeply and focused my will on getting us over the wall. Carefully. I didn't want to catapult us into matching head injuries. "Wrap us in bubble/to keep us from trouble."

An invisible barrier formed around me. My feet lifted off the ground and I strangled the scream in my throat. I needed to stay calm. Millie rose beside me in her bubble, brushing gently against the inflatable material as we headed over the top. I kept my eyes open in case there was a lava pit or a lion's den on the other side of the wall. There wasn't.

It was worse.

We stood on a platform with two rows of poles in front of us. The poles dangled above an oval pool of boiling water. It reminded me of a giant cauldron. Steam drifted upward, frizzing the ends of my hair. Freezing this water would be useless. The drop was so far down that we wouldn't be able to get back up to the surface.

"More water?" Millie groaned. "My palms are too sweaty to grab the poles. I'll never make it across."

"Same here." And the poles were smooth. We'd slide right down into the frothing water below.

Millie exhaled loudly. "Okay, we have to approach this like witches. Lady Weatherby wants us to use magic to get out of the maze, not brute strength."

"Any suggestions? You have more experience thinking like a witch than I do." I was still coming to grips with the fact that I *was* a witch.

Millie scrutinized the dangling poles. "If we can use magic to bend the poles together, they'll form a stirrup."

"Spell's bells, Millie," I said, sounding like a real witch. "That's brilliant. Then we can step across." We'd still need to be careful, but our chances were far better than trying to grip the poles and risk sliding into oblivion.

She whipped out her wand and pointed it at the poles. "What rhymes with stirrup?"

"Not much," I admitted. "Try one that doesn't rhyme."

Millie looked uncertain. "Maybe you should do it. You're better at that than I am."

Wow. A compliment from Millie. Where was my calendar? "I'm happy to try."

I stepped forward and brandished my wand. "Poles to stirrups will carry us across this treacherous path."

The poles began to creak and bend. We watched in disbelief as the two rows reached toward each other and melded together to form a row of U shapes.

Millie moved to the edge, ready to go.

"Take your time," I said. "The poles are still smooth. It would be easy for a foot to slip."

"Same to you," she replied. She gripped the sides and hoisted herself onto the first stirrup. I waited until she was a third of the way across before I followed.

"I hope the other girls are having an easier time," I said, struggling to ignore the boiling water below. Sweat oozed from every pore. I couldn't wait to take a shower later.

I breathed a sigh of relief when Millie made it to the other side.

"Only three more," she said encouragingly.

I placed my foot in one stirrup, and then another.

When I reached the other side, I longed to collapse in a heap.

"Come on, Emma," Millie said. "We can do it."

We pushed through a set of inflatable doors and sunlight washed over us. Momentarily blinded, I tripped and fell to my knees directly in front of a familiar set of pointy, black shoes.

"Congratulations," Lady Weatherby said. "You finished more quickly than I expected."

Millie helped me to my feet. The other girls were already outside.

"I guess we didn't win," I said. I hoped Millie didn't blame me for the loss.

Lady Weatherby looked down her straight nose at me. "On the contrary. I think we can agree that you are all winners today. Class dismissed."

In one swift movement, she took off on her broomstick before I had a chance to ask a follow-up question.

"You were in there forever," Begonia said. "What happened?"

"You mean aside from the scalding pool of water and the impassable wall?" I asked.

Begonia blinked. "Really? Ours was just an inflatable obstacle course. It was fun. I got to bludgeon Sophie with one of those foam mallets."

Millie and I exchanged glances. So this whole ordeal had been for our benefit.

"I didn't say a word," I said quietly. I didn't want Millie to think I'd reported her.

"I know you didn't," Millie said. "Lady Weatherby has a way of knowing things, though. You'll see."

"Truce?" I asked.

Millie hesitated. "Thanks for not snitching. I'm sorry I ruined your date with Demetrius. I didn't know exactly when the spell would kick in."

"You didn't ruin it at all," I said. "And I burned the voodoo doll, by the way."

"Probably for the best."

"Definitely for the best," I said. "Except for the acorn boobs, she looked nothing like me."

CHAPTER 12

ON THURSDAY EVENING, I found myself back at the church for another hour of harp therapy. Thanks to the cookie incident on Tuesday, I hadn't had much opportunity to gather information on Jolene.

"Emma Hart, what a pleasant surprise. Please come in."

I was thrilled to recognize the lilting voice of Maeve McCullen. The stars were in alignment.

"Nice to see you again, Ms. McCullen," I said.

"Do call me Maeve. Are you here to play?" Her strawberry blond ringlets were as perfectly coiled as I remembered.

"I came on Tuesday and really enjoyed it," I said. I omitted the part about the cookies. "Since I have you in front of me, can I ask you a quick question?" No one seemed to be paying us any attention so it seemed safe.

"Sure," Maeve replied. "Fire away."

"Can you see ghosts?"

She twirled a piece of hair around her finger. "Of course, I'm a banshee. Spellbound is full of ghosts."

Yet I'd only seen Gareth.

I dropped my voice. "Would it be possible for you to drop by my house one day, when you're not too busy? There's someone who'd like a word with you."

Maeve eyed me curiously. "You can communicate with Gareth?"

I nodded.

"How interesting." She gazed into my eyes like she was searching for something. "I would love to come and see him. I was terribly fond of Gareth."

"He says the same about you."

A church bell clanged. "Time to get started, everyone," Maeve said.

"There's an empty seat next to me," a woman said, waving me over. Jolene's former seat, presumably.

"You look familiar," I said to the woman as I sat down beside her. Her skin looked as weathered as my grandmother's leather purse, the one she carried every day until her death.

"Phoebe Minor," she said. "We're neighbors."

"Of course." Phoebe was a harpy—sister of Marisol and daughter of Octavia, the sharp-tongued matriarch.

"I've been meaning to drop by and introduce myself," Phoebe said. "Time gets away from me."

In Spellbound, residents had nothing *but* time. "I think you were at the Shamrock Casino when I stopped by to introduce myself."

Phoebe nodded, busily strumming her harp strings. "I'm a regular there. Those leprechauns know a thing or two about customer service."

"I'll have to make it over there one of these days," I said. I'd never been to a casino in the human world. I never had enough money to gamble any away in the name of fun.

"Witches don't usually show an interest in harps," Phoebe said. "Just that weirdo Paisley."

So Phoebe's tongue was as sharp as the rest of her family's. The radiation didn't fall far from the nuclear plant.

"Why don't witches like harps?" I asked.

"It's not about the harp. It's that they stick to themselves," the woman on the other side of Phoebe said. She was built like a boulder with the face only a blind mother could love. "Good to meet you. I'm Sheena Stone."

Stone. I recognized the name. "Are you related to Wayne?" Wayne was another council member as well as an accountant.

"I'm his sister," she said.

That explained it. Sheena was a troll.

"Well, I've met so many interesting people," I said. Okay, not exactly *people*. "It seems silly to stick to the coven."

Sheena seemed to like my answer. "That was Jolene's attitude too."

I grabbed the opportunity. "Jolene, the werewolf?"

Sheena nodded. "The pack tends to be insular, but Jolene wanted to mix with everyone. She loved coming here."

Phoebe shushed her. "That's enough, Sheena. Emma doesn't want to be reminded that she's sitting in the chair of a dead werewolf."

"I don't mind," I said. "Did you know Jolene well?"

"Well enough," Sheena said.

"You need to look at your sheet music," Phoebe said. "You won't learn anything if you just sit here yammering."

Actually, there was a chance I'd learn everything I wanted to know if we sat here yammering, but I could see that was too risky.

The troll seemed less interested in being judgmental and more interested in being helpful. A good sign.

"I don't know how to read music," I admitted.

"Then how do you expect to play an instrument?" Phoebe snapped.

Sheena jumped to the rescue. "I can help you, dear."

"Thanks, Sheena," I said. "That would be great."

Sheena shot the harpy a triumphant look. I had a feeling those two were competitive over more than my approval.

"I guess Jolene was getting excited about her wedding," I said, careful to keep my tone casual.

"Who knows?" Phoebe said. "The girl talked about as much as a mute."

"Not true," Sheena said. "She just didn't talk to *you*. She didn't trust you not to blab to your family."

"Was there something to do with the wedding that she didn't want people to know?" I asked.

"For one thing, she didn't want a whole big affair," Sheena said. "She didn't like the whole pack coming to witness the ceremony."

"She said she wanted it to be more intimate," another voice chimed in.

"That's right," Sheena said. "You spoke to her about it, didn't you?" Sheena jerked her head toward the young woman. "This one can tell you. Emma, meet Susie. They compared wedding notes every week."

"I was married last year," Susie said. She sighed blissfully. "Still feels like yesterday."

I scooted my chair over toward the newlywed. "So what did you two compare notes about?"

"Why?" Phoebe asked. "Thinking about getting married soon?"

"I just love weddings," I enthused. A bald-faced lie. I avoided weddings like the plague, usually because I didn't have a date and didn't want to go alone.

"Too bad there won't be one," Phoebe said. "Not that you'd get invited to a pack wedding. They're strict about outsiders attending anything related to the pack."

I focused my attention on Susie. "I bet Jolene was really looking forward to life with Alex," I said. "He's one good-looking guy."

The sound of swooning swirled in the air. All of the women's expressions grew dreamy.

"Alex is a slice of beefcake I'd like a bite of," Phoebe growled. Not what I was expecting to hear from the older harpy.

"Did Jolene have any competition for Alex's affections?" I asked.

"Hard to say," Sheena said. "Once the pack made it clear they intended for him to marry Jolene, nobody had the chutzpah to make a play for him."

"He never would have married outside the pack anyway," Susie said. "Alex is a leader, but he respects the rules."

"So not even another shifter?" I asked. I wasn't sure how many types of shifters there were in Spellbound.

"Definitely not," Phoebe scoffed. "Werewolves consider themselves the top of the shifter food chain. For someone like Alex, a wereferret would be unthinkable."

Even though everyone was saying that witches were insular too, I knew for a fact they could marry other supernaturals. It was one of the first questions I'd asked—not that I had anyone in mind, of course. I was only twenty-five.

"I heard Jolene wasn't sure about the marriage," I said. "Is that true?"

"You wouldn't know it from the way she talked

about their future together," Susie said. "She even had names picked out for their three future daughters—Nanette, Babette, and Jeanette."

I winced. "Cute names."

"Ridiculous names," Phoebe spat. "That's one problem avoided thanks to her death."

Having met Octavia, her mother, Phoebe's bitter attitude was hardly surprising.

"Enough chatter," Phoebe said. "Let's get back to the music. It's not like Myra will give us extra time. She's always waiting by that Godforsaken door with the key."

Sheena put a finger to her lips. "Phoebe, we're in a church. It can't possibly be a Godforsaken door."

Distracted by their conversation, I caught my fingernails on the harp's strings and pulled away, creating a cringe-inducing sound.

Phoebe's hands flew to cover her ears. "Someone teach this girl how to play. I'm here to relax. Goodness knows I hear enough screeching in my house."

"Sorry," I said. "Maybe I'll just listen tonight."

"Not as dumb as you look," Phoebe muttered.

Phoebe's abrasive personality aside, I could understand why Jolene liked attending these classes. Although I didn't recognize any of the music I heard, it didn't matter. The soothing sounds put me in a pleasant trance, where my concerns faded to the background. I stopped thinking about Jolene, broomsticks, Daniel—all the worries that plagued me. I was almost catatonic by the end of the session.

"We'll see you next week," Sheena said, giving me a gentle shake.

I blinked and looked around the room. Nearly everyone was gone.

"Did I fall asleep?" I asked.

"Not exactly," she said with a smile. "We call it the harp hangover. Much more pleasant than the other kind."

It certainly was. Although I'd come here to investigate Jolene's death, I knew I'd be back after the case was resolved. One positive result from a negative situation. On the way out of the church, I paused by the altar and silently thanked Jolene for leading me here.

After class the next day, I decided to stop by the bookstore in the town square. It had been years since I'd set foot in a bookstore. In the human world, I read e-books so there was no need.

The store was a comfortable size—not too big, not too small. There were sofas scattered throughout the store, encouraging customers to linger. Juliet was easy to spot. At six foot tall, the Amazon stood out. Her gaze fell upon me, and I saw the flash of recognition in her eyes.

"Miss Hart, I was wondering if I'd ever see you in here," she said. She came out from behind the counter to greet me.

"Good afternoon, Miss Montlake," I said. "I'm sorry it's taken me this long. I loved to read in the human world, but here I've only had time for law books."

"And what are you interested in finding here?"

"Do you have any books on the history of the town and its residents?" I asked. Werewolf pack culture and Linsey's case had highlighted the gaping hole in my general paranormal knowledge. "I thought it might be handy to keep a copy at home so that I can read up on it when I have spare time." A library book would be due back long before I could finish it.

"There are a few options," she said, steering me toward the nonfiction section. "The two most popular titles are in here." She plucked two books off a middle shelf. "This one was written by a wizard named Theodore Dazzle. The other was written by a vampire called Lazarus. No last name."

So he was the Madonna of the vampire set. "Are they both still living?"

"I'm afraid not," she said. "Theodore died of old age, which is rare, but it happens. Lazarus died during an argument with a werewolf many years ago."

"That must've been one serious argument," I said.

"A sad state of affairs, really," she said. "Before that happened, the different species in town seemed to be working well together. After Lazarus died, the pack closed ranks. That's when they started carving out territory in the Pines and the other forested areas."

"Oh, I had assumed it was always like that."

"It seems to only be getting worse," Juliet said sadly. "The ordinances haven't done us any favors. It's only appeased the residents who complained about shifting and trespassing in the first place."

"The vocal minority," I said. Yes, we had plenty of that in the human world as well.

Juliet handed me the books. "Take them," she said. "No charge."

"I can't do that," I said. "You won't be able to stay in business if you give books away for free."

"This store is a labor of love. If I want to give away books, I'm perfectly happy to do so." Her focus shifted to a different section of the store. "While you're here, I have a few other books that might be of interest."

Books of interest to me? I was eager to see what she had in mind.

I followed her across the store to the section labeled 'witches and wizards.'

"I have a number of books on covens in particular," she said. "I thought you might be interested in researching your heritage."

I stared at the rows of books in front of me. "I wouldn't even know where to begin," I said. "Other than the fact that I'm a witch, I know nothing about my family's origin."

Juliet clucked her tongue. "You know that your familiar is an owl, rather than a cat. That's not a trait of the local coven."

And I could see ghosts. Still, it didn't give me enough information to go on. "Where would I start? By checking the indexes of each book to see whether they mention owls as familiars?"

This was where technology would come in handy. A simple online search would reveal any covens associated with owls or psychic abilities. Too bad Spellbound wasn't plugged in.

"I suppose it will be labor intensive," she said. "But I would imagine it will be well worth it."

I felt like she was going to tell me that knowledge was its own reward. Unfortunately, my schedule didn't currently allow for rewards like that. Knowledge would have to wait.

"Take these for now," Juliet said. "Come back when you have more time. There are also books in the library that might help you."

"I was told that you know a lot about the town's history," I said. "Have you read all of these history books?"

"I have," Juliet admitted. "As I think I told you when we met in the Great Hall, there are different versions of events, particularly surrounding the curse itself. The accounts in these books cover what came immediately after. If you look hard enough, though, there are clues to the curse."

"Does no one care?" I asked. "Shouldn't there be a team devoted to teasing out this information and breaking the curse?"

"It's become a story," she explained. "People nowadays tend to treat it like a fable. Or a fairytale. A way of explaining our existence here."

I understood that well. Humans had been doing

the same for centuries. "Do you believe there's a way to break the curse?"

"I would never say it's impossible," she said. "I suppose most of us are simply content here. Life is good in Spellbound for the most part. There's no incentive to break the curse."

Tell that to Daniel and Jolene.

"But you think I have an incentive, don't you?"

Juliet smiled. "I think you've proven yourself to be smart and capable and not from this world. If anyone is to discover a way out, I don't think it would be unreasonable to bet on you."

"I think you overestimate me, Miss Montlake," I said. "I'm in survival mode here. I'm just trying to get by. I don't have time for any high-level thinking."

"Survival mode, indeed. All the more reason to find a way out." She waved to a quick customer at the front of the store. "If you'll excuse me, someone else requires assistance. Nice to see you again. Don't be a stranger."

"Thanks for the books," I said. The only incentive I had right now was to make it through the next week. Breaking the curse wasn't even on the list. Still, it would be smart to read about the town's history. I needed to understand the pack, as well as some of the other paranormal dynamics.

CHAPTER 13

THE DAY of Linsey's trial was here.

We stepped into the Great Hall, which apparently doubled as a courtroom in Spellbound. I found out the morning of the trial that the judge would be Hester Longbottom. The process seemed fairly informal considering the young berserker's future was on the line. When I raised the issue with Gareth, he appeared unconcerned.

"Anything special I need to know about Judge Longbottom aside from her son's tragic history?" I'd asked before I left the house.

"She has a pet koala that she likes to dress in outfits." Not what I was expecting to hear.

Gareth had also suggested that Linsey dye her hair back to its natural color and lose the makeup for the day of trial. In the human world, the suggestion would've been the same. I decided to let Linsey be Linsey, however. Her outrageous look supported her outrageous behavior. She was a teenager acting out and a berserker to boot, and nothing more. Her actions did not suggest a future life of crime. I hoped Judge Longbottom saw it the same way.

I met Linsey in the lobby of the Great Hall. As instructed, she wore her usual black attire, combat boots, and obnoxious jewelry and makeup.

"How are you feeling?" I asked.

"Hopeful," she said. It was a good word. A word I wanted to hear. It meant that she hadn't given up on herself.

"What about your parents? Are they coming?" It would look better if the parents were in attendance.

Linsey shook her head. "We're still not on speaking terms," she said. "Maybe after the trial, they'll come around."

I only hoped by then it wasn't too late. If I didn't do my job well, they would be visiting their daughter in prison. That thought did not sit well with me.

The double doors opened and an elf summoned us inside. This would be my second time in the Great Hall. The first time was my very first night in Spellbound. This room was where the council had informed me that I couldn't leave town because I was a witch. Talk about a shock. I tried not to get distracted by the memory. I was here to defend Linsey. I had to focus on that.

Judge Longbottom sat alone on a raised platform behind a table. It was not as intimate as an American courtroom. The room was far too large for that. And grand.

"Good morning, Miss Hart."

"Good morning, Judge Longbottom," I said. "This is my first case, so I hope you'll go easy on me."

"I should think you're more interested in me being easy on your client," she said.

I winced. Not the best start to the trial.

Linsey and I sat together at a table in front of the platform. Adjacent to us sat Rochester, the prosecuting attorney. I smiled in greeting, but he didn't smile back.

"We will endeavor to dispense of this case quickly," the judge said. "The prosecutor has a noon tee time and I have a dental appointment."

It was good to know that justice was on a schedule.

"We see no reason why we can't reach a satisfying conclusion, Your Honor," I said. "My client has already pled guilty, so we are simply asking for leniency in her sentencing."

"The average sentence for vandalism is usually one year imprisonment. Are you aware of that?" The judge peered at me over her glasses. For a brief moment, it struck me funny that a werepanther required glasses. I thought cats were known for their eyesight, particularly large cats.

"I have familiarized myself with the sentencing guidelines for vandalism," I said. "But I would like to remind the court that Linsey is only eighteen years old. We've all made mistakes in our youth that we regret. She has offered to repair the damage done to Fern's jalopy. In my conversations with her, she has shown remorse."

"And what about her condition the night of the crime?" the prosecutor asked. "Are we to ignore the use of illicit substances and the poor judgment she showed in running through town in nothing but a wolf pelt?"

"The pack has lodged a complaint about the wolf pelt," the judge said. "But that's a matter for another day."

"My client agrees to relinquish the wolf pelt," I said. I heard a whimper of protest beside me and quickly stamped on Linsey's boot. If a sacrifice was needed in order to secure her freedom, then so be it. The wolf pelt was the least of it.

"Miss Hart, what makes you so certain that your client's actions were simply a youthful indiscretion and that we won't be seeing her back in this room in another year for another, more serious crime?"

"Because I have spent time with my client, Your Honor. I find her behavior to be typical for someone her age. I also think she lacked the guidance that she has sorely needed up until now. I'm not sure if you noticed from the artwork on the jalopy, but my client happens to be a very talented artist. I'm hopeful that we can channel that talent into more productive uses."

"I agree that she is talented," the prosecutor said. "The images on the vehicle were—ahem—very realistic."

The judge sat back in her chair, thinking. "So what do you suggest, Miss Hart?"

"I suggest no time served," I said. "My client is more than willing to do community service for the year. I would like to recommend that the community service tap into her artistic talents. Maybe working in an art class with children," I said.

The wizard beside me erupted. "I object, Your Honor. Let this wayward youth influence children even younger than her? Outrageous."

"What's the problem, counselor?" I asked. "Are

you afraid she's going to teach them how to draw naughty images?"

The judge didn't appear as outraged by the suggestion. She focused on Linsey. "Young lady, what do you have to say for yourself?"

Linsey stood and met the judge's inquisitive gaze. "I am very sorry for the trouble I caused, ma'am. It was a lapse in judgment. One I promise not to repeat. Miss Hart is right. I haven't had appropriate guidance, but I am not going to blame my actions on that. I want to do better. I want to be better. I know there are people in Spellbound who can help me do that. I would love the opportunity to work in the community. Miss Hart said I need direction and I think she's right."

My heart swelled with pride. She sounded like...a grown-up.

"I am pleased to hear that you're taking responsibility for your actions," the judge said. "I am inclined to take Miss Hart's suggestion."

The wizard jumped to his feet. "Your Honor, I beg you. At least a six month sentence or we risk setting a bad precedent."

"For vandalism?" I said. "Really? She didn't destroy the car. It can be repainted easily enough. She has offered to do it, or to pay for it. She would also like to apologize to Fern in person. We only want to do that if the victim is willing, however."

The judge nodded, satisfied. "All right then. One year of community service. I would like Linsey to start her adult life with a clean record." She banged her gavel on the table. "Case dismissed."

Linsey's arms were around me before I had time to stand. "Thank you," she said. I heard the shaky emotion in her voice.

"I meant every word, Linsey. I want to find a way to help you hone your talent and find your place in this town. Everyone needs to find her place here, including me."

Linsey looked at me and smiled. "I think you already have."

CHAPTER 14

THERE WAS no time to revel in my first court victory —not when my broomstick final was the next morning. I couldn't bring myself to leave the comfort of my bed.

Gareth was having none of it. "Kip's over. Get up or I'll tell Magpie to stand on your chest. His morning breath is one thing I don't miss."

"Do that and I'll start inviting the harpies over for weekly tea."

He groaned. "It's for your own good. You've got your solo flight today."

"Stop following my schedule," I grumbled, yanking the covers back over my head.

"I really need to find a way to move tangible objects," Gareth said. "It would open all kinds of doors for me. I mean, I could literally open doors."

"It's good to have goals," I said. I continued to grip the covers over my head. I just didn't feel ready to face the day.

"What's the worst that can happen?" he asked. "You christen the head of your professor with puke? So what? It's nothing you haven't done before."

"You're not helping," my muffled voice said.

"You're not going to die," he insisted. "I know it seems that way. I promise you, your witchy friends won't let anything happen to you. In all the years I've been here, I've never heard of a witch dying on her broomstick."

"That's because she'd already fallen off," I said.

"Hardy har."

"Just the thought of being so high in the air makes me nauseous," I said. I pulled back the covers so that I could see Gareth.

"You're still taking the anti-anxiety potion, aren't you?" he asked. "I saw the bottle in the bathroom."

"Stop snooping," I demanded.

"I can't help it if you leave your things everywhere," he said indignantly.

"I leave my things everywhere because it's my house," I said. "My things are supposed to be everywhere."

"I'll tell you what," he said. "You get through today and I will reward you."

I cast a sidelong glance at him. "You'll reward me how?" How could a ghost reward me? It wasn't like he could bake me cookies.

He rubbed his hands together eagerly. "I don't know yet," he said. "I swear on my life, it will be something good."

I folded my arms across my chest. "On your life? You need to do better than that."

"Fine," he huffed. "I promise to tell you one of Spellbound's best kept secrets."

Now he was speaking my language. I flipped back the covers and hopped out of bed.

"What's a good outfit for a solo broomstick ride?"

"Obviously not a dress," he said. "Unless you think flashing Professor Holmes will give you extra marks."

"I'll stick to pants, thanks."

Now that I'd decided to go through with it, I needed to hustle. I was already nervous. Add tardiness to the mix and I'd be tight ball of nerves by the time I got there.

"You're bringing Sedgwick, right?" he asked.

"I can't decide if that would be a help or a hindrance," I said.

Hey, I'm right here, Sedgwick said.

I looked around and saw him perched on top of the dresser.

"Get your bird off my expensive furniture," Gareth cried.

Sedgwick continued to perch there, oblivious to Gareth's protests.

Daniel waited for me in the kitchen with a bowl of porridge sprinkled with cinnamon and a dash of confidence. The dash of confidence was a nice touch, but just having Gareth and Daniel on my side made a huge difference.

"Do you want me to fly you over there so you're not late?" Daniel offered.

"No, thanks. If Professor Holmes sees you, he'll feel like he has to report you." He wasn't out of the woods yet.

I hurried outside. It didn't help that I had to walk all the way to the field where the broomstick session would be held. If nothing else, I was getting good exercise.

Everyone was there waiting when I arrived. Begonia shot me a look of concern.

"I was afraid you weren't coming," she whispered.

"I did consider it," I said. "But sometimes we have

to do things we don't want to do. Part of growing up."

"I'm sure you'll do great," Sophie said. "You've been working really hard."

"Unfortunately, hard work doesn't always breed success," I replied. It was one of those rules I hated to learn, but it was a universal truth that could not be ignored.

Professor Holmes gave me a curt nod before calling Millie to the front. She took her place on the broom and completed all of the required maneuvers in record time. Professor Holmes seemed immensely pleased with her performance. Naturally, nobody wanted to follow her.

"Miss Hart," Professor Holmes said. "You're up."

"Me?" I squeaked. I was expecting to go last.

"You are the only Miss Hart here, I believe."

I took a step forward and the professor handed me his broom.

"Good luck," Begonia called.

I gripped the handle of the broomstick and walked over to the clearing. I tried to focus my will, but my insides were churning. My anxiety was so high right now, though, I wasn't sure even magic potion could help me.

I swung one leg over the broomstick and placed

myself three quarters of the way back the way I'd been taught. It still didn't feel natural to me, nor did I think it ever would. Even so, I knew I had to clear this hurdle. As much as I loved my classmates, I didn't want to be a remedial witch forever. Heck, I didn't want to be a witch at all, but no one gave me a choice in the matter. Like being short. Maybe you want to be tall, but your DNA has other plans.

I forced myself keep my eyes open despite the constant urge to squeeze them shut. I mustered my courage and said, "I was born for the sky/now watch me fly." The broom lurched once before vaulting me into the air. I desperately tried to keep both hands on the broomstick this time.

I rose higher and higher, my anxiety rising with every foot.

Watch out for that bird. Sedgwick's voice jolted me.

"Are you out of your mind? Do you want me to die?" I glanced over my shoulder at the spotted owl flying beside me. "Forget it. Don't answer that."

You're still airborne, he said. *That's progress, right?*

I kept my gaze on Sedgwick as he flew slightly in front of me. It helped for me to have somewhere to focus my attention. Otherwise, I'd be tempted to look down. I definitely did not want to look down.

We're flying over the academy, he told me. *Oh look,*

there's Lady Weatherby now. He swiveled his head one hundred and eighty degrees to look at me. *If you're going to vomit, now would be an excellent time.*

"Sedgwick, you're horrible." I glanced below. "It is Lady Weatherby, isn't it?" Even from this distance, I recognized the distinctive headdress with the twisted horns.

Don't get distracted, Sedgwick warned.

I forced my attention back to the owl. "I thought you wanted to see me fail," I said. "Isn't that how you get your jollies?"

There are a million ways to amuse myself, he said. *Humiliating you is only one of them.*

"I need to do the first maneuver now," I said. I knew the clock was ticking. I had to complete the set in ten minutes or less. Otherwise, it was considered a failure.

I'm rooting for you to get your broomstick license so you can deliver your own messages, Sedgwick said. *Let's go.*

I fixed my attention on the owl as he banked a sharp left. I quickly followed suit. I managed the turn without sliding off this time. Success!

The next maneuver was a steep climb. Sedgwick went vertical, and so did I. Nausea rolled over me, but I stayed the course. My hair blew back and the temperature seemed to drop five degrees. I leveled off to prepare for the next maneuver.

You're halfway done, Sedgwick said. It was the most encouraging he'd ever sounded.

The third maneuver was the loop-de-loop.

My eyes desperately wanted to close. They did not want to witness seeing Spellbound from any angle at this height, but certainly not while upside down.

Sedgwick circled up and over. I didn't stop to think. I just did it.

I heard the cheers from the ground and knew that I'd done it successfully. I couldn't bring myself to look at them, though. It was too much of a risk.

Only one maneuver left. The landing. It could still go wrong if I stopped focusing.

This part is all you, Sedgwick said. He flew off and I concentrated on the final maneuver. Some witches found landing to be the easiest part. For me, there was no easy part.

I pictured a giant X on the ground. As I moved my gaze from the sky to the field below, another wave of nausea slammed into me. I fought hard to maintain control.

"I can do this," I whispered to myself. The

soothing sounds of a harp drifted through my brain and I instantly relaxed.

My gaze flickered to my friends on the ground, their expressions eager and supportive. I couldn't let them down.

I steered the broomstick to the invisible landing strip and glided to the ground.

"Nine minutes and fifty seconds," Professor Holmes announced. "Congratulations, Miss Hart. You've earned yourself a broom."

I dropped to my knees and kissed the soft earth before vomiting all over it.

"I don't think Jolene killed herself," I announced.

Begonia and Sophie had insisted on going to the Horned Owl for drinks to celebrate my broomstick victory and my first successful trial.

"What makes you so certain?" Sophie asked.

I filled them in on harp therapy and the anti-depression potion. By all accounts, Jolene was ready to embrace the next chapter in her life.

"So if she didn't kill herself and Daniel is innocent, who's next on the list?" Begonia asked.

I lowered my voice. "What about Lorenzo Mancini?"

"You can't possibly be serious," Sophie said. "Mancini is the head of the pack. He might kill you for making that accusation."

"The pack isn't the mob," I said. "I'm not making an accusation. I'm just throwing it out there as a possibility."

"What could he possibly have to gain from Jolene's death?" Begonia asked. "He's already the head of the pack and he has a wife."

"Do you think Lorenzo and Jolene were having an affair?" Sophie asked, her eyes wide.

"No. Maybe it's simple revenge," I said. "Everyone seems to expect that Alex will take over the pack when Lorenzo dies. Maybe I'm Lorenzo and I hear this. I start to feel a little anxious. Maybe even a little annoyed that people seem to think my time is coming to an end. Do I kill Alex directly? Maybe. Or maybe I weaken him by taking away something important. His mate."

The other witches stared at me. Sophie took a long, slow sip of her pomegranate pom-pom.

"Your mind goes to dark places," Begonia said.

"I was a public interest lawyer in the human world, don't forget. Unfortunately, I glimpsed a lot of dark places in my short adult life."

The bartender signaled that the rest of our drinks were ready.

"I'll get them," Sophie volunteered.

"But you already have your drink," I said. In fact, she was the only one.

Begonia leaned forward and whispered, "Sophie has a crush on the bartender."

Sophie elbowed her friend in the ribs. "I do not."

I craned my neck for another look at the bartender. He was handsome in a scruffy sort of way. "What is he?"

"His name is Ty," Sophie said. "He's a satyr."

"Isn't he a little old for you?" I asked. Although I wasn't that much older than Sophie, I felt protective of her.

"You mean as opposed to an angel or a vampire?" Begonia asked good-naturedly.

She had a point. "Go on then," I urged Sophie.

She looked at us uneasily. "Do I look okay? Do I need a quick beauty spell?"

"Don't be silly," Begonia said. "You're adorable."

Sophie slid out of the booth and walked casually to the bar to collect the drinks. I watched as she made an effort to interact with the bartender. Unfortunately, his attention had been drawn to a sultry nymph at the opposite end of the bar.

"Maybe we should do a boob spell on Sophie," Begonia said.

"Bite your tongue," I said. "Sophie doesn't want to attract someone with her physical appearance. She wants him to be interested in her mind, in her good nature."

"Yeah, but being attractive helps."

Sadly, I couldn't argue with that.

Sophie returned with the drinks, looking forlorn. "Well, that didn't go well. Bitsy appeared at precisely the wrong time."

"Bitsy is the nymph?" I asked.

Sophie nodded. "She seems to frequent the bars and restaurants in town. She'll date someone for about a year and then move on to the next target."

"Why bars and restaurants?" I asked.

"She's a groupie," Begonia said. "And she loves the free food and drinks."

"I don't think she's paid for a meal in decades," Sophie added.

The nymph was draped across the bar top, batting her eyes at Ty. I had a feeling that Sophie didn't stand a chance.

"Don't worry, Sophie," I said. "We'll find someone who appreciates you."

"It's okay," Sophie said glumly. She stared into the

bottom of her glass. "Mom and dad say my priority needs to be graduation. I can't let myself get distracted by boys."

"I'm trying to do the same," I said. "And that's what I told Demetrius."

Begonia's fingers encircled my wrist and she squeezed hard. "What are you telling me? You broke up with Demetrius Hunt?"

"Not exactly," I said. Inasmuch as you can't break up with someone you aren't actually dating.

"Is this because of someone else?" Sophie asked.

"Of course not," I insisted. "Between a new job, witch training, and adjusting to this whole new life, I don't think it makes sense for me to get involved with anyone right now. There's plenty of time for that."

"I, for one, think you're insane," Begonia said.

Sophie's eyes bulged. "Don't look now. But Lorenzo Mancini just walked into the pub."

"Really? Maybe I should go and speak with him," I said. Both girls reached out and gripped my arms.

"You really are insane," Begonia said. "You do not want to get on the wrong side of the pack. That's a bad idea for anyone, especially someone new like you."

"It's just a friendly conversation," I said. "If I do it right, he won't even know what I'm up to."

"Lorenzo is smart," Sophie said. "He'll figure out what you're doing inside of a minute."

I shrugged. "Worth a shot."

"Whatever you do, don't get straight to the point," Sophie said. "Werewolves tend to feel challenged by directness."

"Don't worry," I said. "I won't go there."

I slid out of the seat and sauntered over to Lorenzo's table. He was alone, already with a drink in hand. No surprise that he received VIP treatment.

He gave me a polite smile as I approached.

"Miss Hart, good to see you taking advantage of the Spellbound watering holes. You seem to be settling in rather well."

"May I sit? Or are you waiting for someone?"

He gestured for me to sit down. "You seem to have found your own pack," he said, with a brief nod in the direction of Sophie and Begonia. "It's important in life to find your people."

"You've been leader of your pack quite a long time," I said. "Your people must be very special to you. They're like your children."

"To call them children is a bit patronizing," he

said. "I prefer to think of myself as everyone's stronger, wiser brother."

So his ego didn't seem to be at issue. Much.

"Any news on Jolene?" I asked. I was careful to avoid the word murder.

His expression turned grim. "No new leads as of yet," he said. "I have some members investigating as well. We can't leave these things to Sheriff Hugo. The sheriff is a good centaur, but he likes his puzzles to be simple. And so he tries to make them so. As you and I both know, however, life doesn't always work that way."

We were in total agreement on that point.

"Does it bother you that members say Alex is your natural successor? Does that make you feel like they're ready for a regime change?" Okay, so I went there.

Lorenzo's eyes turned golden. I recognized that look. The wolf within. So I guess it did bother him.

"I would be lying if I denied it. Show me a man who likes to contemplate his own demise."

I bit back a smile. I could show him one right now. In fact, he was probably in his thinking spot at this very moment, contemplating his own demise.

"Do you like Alex?" I asked.

"Miss Hart, if I didn't know any better, I would

say that you are attempting to interrogate me." He picked up his drink and drained the glass. It was purposeful, like he was trying to control the flow of the conversation.

"Sooner or later, I'm going to be defending someone," I said. "Questions like these are going to come up. Best to get them answered now."

"I do appreciate your devotion to your new position." He wiped his mouth with his napkin. "I wish everyone in town showed such dedication and tenacity."

"You haven't answered my question."

"Yes, of course I like Alex. Everyone likes Alex. Why do you think I put him in a position to rise in the ranks?"

"What do you mean?"

"I gave Alex his first promotion," Lorenzo said. "Over many objections I might add. His father Duke and his mother LuAnn are not particularly respected in the pack. The other wolves in my retinue weren't sure about Alex, but I believed in him. I still believe in him."

I hadn't realized that. I thought Alex's rise was due to popularity in the pack, not because Lorenzo supported him. I still had a lot to learn about the inner workings of Spellbound.

"What about Jolene?" I asked. "What were your feelings about her?"

"Her father was one of my best friends before his death," he said. "I pushed for the match."

"I was under the impression that everyone supported the match initially, except Alex and Jolene."

"We do try to keep information within the pack," Lorenzo said. "Makes us look weak when we can't agree."

The more I talked with Lorenzo, the more I liked him. Although he was intimidating with his slick appearance and his wolfish gaze, I found myself warming to him.

"You do realize it's quite dangerous to accuse a council member of a serious offense," he said, although I was pretty sure I detected a trace of amusement.

"I wouldn't dream of accusing you of anything, Mr. Mancini," I said. "Unlike some residents here, I am not suicidal."

He chuckled. "To be blunt, I did not kill Jolene. I fully support Alex as my future successor. And now I have to go to the trouble of finding Alex a new mate. To be crass, it's a huge inconvenience to the pack. It creates uncertainty and no one likes uncertainty. Our members get restless."

"Thank you, Mr. Mancini. I do appreciate you being candid with me."

"Consider this your free pass, Miss Hart. The next time you disrespect me like this, make no mistake, there will be consequences."

My insides twisted. So maybe warming to him was a bit premature.

I nodded and left the table. Begonia and Sophie awaited my return in silence. I noticed they were clutching hands. They must've been truly nervous for me.

"Well, the good news is that I don't think Lorenzo is our man," I said, dropping into my seat.

"No, the good news is that you're still alive," Begonia said.

Truer words were never spoken.

CHAPTER 15

When we left the Horned Owl, I had the distinct feeling we were being watched.

"What's wrong?" Sophie asked, noticing my apprehension.

I stopped walking. "Wait here a second." I turned left and walked toward a tall, shadowy figure behind a fey lantern pole.

"Astrid?" I queried. "Are you hiding?" I couldn't imagine what else the imposing Valkyrie was doing behind the pole.

The deputy stepped into the light. "Not hiding." She peered over her shoulder. "Okay, maybe hiding a little bit. I don't want the sheriff to know I'm sharing information with you."

I cocked my head. "You're sharing information with me?"

"I liked how you handled the situation with Mumford and, between you and me, I know Daniel would never kill anyone." She glanced warily at Begonia and Sophie. "Tell your friends to keep walking."

I waved the girls on. "I'll speak to you later," I called, and turned back to Astrid. "So what's the information?"

"This way," she said. "I know somewhere private we can talk."

"My office is close by," I said. "We can go there."

"Nope, sorry. I like Althea, but I don't trust her not to mention my visit to one of her sisters."

Although Althea wouldn't be there at this hour, I didn't argue.

We walked around the block and ended up in front of the library.

"Perfect," I said. "I've been meaning to stop by here."

In the lobby of the building was an atrium where I could see multiples floors of bookshelves all around us.

"There's a section on the third floor where no one ever goes," Astrid said.

I followed her to a staircase and we trudged to the third floor. "No magical elevator?"

"Oh, there are faster ways. I just like the exercise."

"Remind me to check out the children's section before we leave," I said.

She arched an eyebrow. "Something you need to tell me?"

I blushed. "No, of course not. There's a book I'd like to check out for a friend." I wasn't about to share the details of my Winnie the Pooh conversation with Daniel. It was too personal.

Astrid leaned on a shelf between stacks of books about the insect world. "They found silver in her bloodstream."

Silver? "How?"

"Colloidal silver is available in several shops in town," the Valkyrie said. "I'm looking into its origin."

"But she was a werewolf," I said.

"Exactly." Astrid leaned forward. "I think she was poisoned."

"Why is suicide ruled out?" I asked. "Wouldn't poisoning herself be a less violent way to go?"

"Because it wasn't one lethal dose. Based on the autopsy results, it built up in her system over time. There's a good chance she didn't know she was ingesting it."

The gears began clicking in my mind. Someone had poisoned her. "Alex?"

Astrid pressed her lips together. "It doesn't look good for him."

"The marriage was arranged," I said. "Lorenzo pushed for Jolene."

"Maybe Alex never really accepted it," Astrid said.

Because he was headstrong and fiercely independent or because he disliked his intended mate?

"Does Sheriff Hugo think Daniel poisoned her with silver?" I asked.

"No, but he won't come out and say it. He's a stubborn centaur. That's why I came to you, my human friend." She cleared her throat. "Sorry, my witch friend."

I smiled. "Calling me a human is not an insult," I assured her. At least not to me. "Is he planning to question Alex with this new information?"

"Yes," she replied. "But not until the morning."

"Why the delay?"

Astrid made a disapproving face. "It's his poker night."

I guess that's the attitude you can afford to have when you have a job for life. A very long life.

"Who does he play poker with?" I was curious to know who the sheriff's cronies were—so that I could avoid them.

"Frank. He's the gnome who owns the Enchanted

Garden." She ticked the rest off on her fingers. "Lord Gilder. Stan, the town registrar. Boyd. A few other occasional players."

"You don't play poker?" I asked.

Her expression darkened. "Doesn't matter if I did. Boys only."

Wow. Sexism was alive and well in the cursed town of Spellbound.

"We should start our own poker club," I said.

"It's not a club. Just a weekly game."

I knew nothing about poker. "Okay, so let's have a game night. Girls only. Who can we invite?"

A slow smile emerged. "Are you serious?"

"Why not? Lucy will join us." I sensed that, beneath her sweet fairy exterior, Lucy could be quite competitive.

"Lucy would be awesome. What about your classmates?"

"I'll invite them. How about tomorrow night at my house?" If all went well, Daniel would be free to leave before then.

"I'll bring the cards." Astrid was practically vibrating with excitement. It seemed she was a fan of poker after all.

"So back to business," I said. "If Sheriff Hugo is

heading to poker soon, I'm guessing it would be a good time for a chat with Alex."

Astrid held up her hands. "What you do in your private time is your business, Miss Hart. If you want to check on Alex and see how he's coping with his loss, I won't stop you."

I winked at her. "You go first so we're not seen together. I'm going to find a couple of books on my way out."

As I walked over to the Pines from the library, I realized how poor my timing was. The sun was low in the sky, casting a pink and orange glow across the horizon.

Is it a full moon tonight, Sedgwick? He was too high to hear me properly, so I used telepathy.

No, tomorrow night, but it doesn't matter. The werewolves won't turn. There's an ordinance, remember?

So there was no cause for alarm, at least where werewolves and other shifters were concerned.

Alex was within view on the front porch as I approached the house, shirtless and working up a sweat with a hammer. His biceps bulged and suddenly the allure of the alpha male became crystal clear.

He stopped and sniffed the air before his gaze alighted on me. "You again. Emma, right?"

"It is." I picked up the pace and caught sight of Sedgwick heading for the rooftop.

Alex set down the hammer and wiped his brow. "What brings you all the way out here at this hour?"

"I just wanted to see how you were doing," I said.

The front door opened and Kayla emerged from the house, carrying a tray with a jug of lemonade and two glasses. Her brow creased when she noticed me.

"Sorry, I didn't realize we had company. I can fetch another glass."

"Don't trouble yourself on my account," I said.

Kayla placed the tray on a small table. "It's no trouble. I'll be right back."

Once she disappeared inside the house, Alex grinned at me. "Werewolf hospitality. Ain't nothing like it."

He swiped a glass from the tray and filled it to the brim with ice-cold lemonade. "It's homemade. Jolene's family recipe. Kayla's keeping the tradition alive." He took a long sip. "Ever little thing reminds me of her."

"I guess you've been trying to keep busy," I said. I

knew what it was like to keep a shattered mind occupied.

"Hands, head, heart." He exhaled loudly. "I've been aiming to keep every bit of me distracted."

Heart? I thought that was an interesting inclusion.

The front door swung open and Kayla thrust a glass into my hand. "Here you go."

Ah, the awkward teenage years. How little I missed them.

"Thanks for coming out to check on us," Kayla said. "Most townsfolk seem to be steering clear like we have a disease or something." She lifted the jug and filled my glass halfway.

"I think it's human nature." I paused. "Or just nature. People don't know how to act, especially when we still don't know what happened to Jolene. Everyone's on edge."

"Well, the sheriff says she killed herself," Kayla said. "Is everyone afraid they're gonna catch suicidal thoughts?"

Alex shot her a hard look. "That's enough, Kayla."

She immediately lowered her head. "Sorry," she mumbled.

"Why don't you take your lemonade inside and leave the adults to talk out here?" Alex said.

Judging by the scowl on her face, Kayla didn't seem to like that suggestion, but she did as she was told. Alex waited until she was in the house to continue the conversation.

"Why do I get the feeling you have something to tell me?" he asked, polishing off his lemonade. "Is it something to do with the angel?"

"No," I said. "Nothing to do with Daniel." Thank goodness. "The sheriff is going to come and see you tomorrow. The lab found traces of silver in Jolene's body." I watched him carefully to gauge his reaction to the news.

"Silver?" he scoffed. "That's impossible. Our systems can't handle silver." He hesitated, his expression shifting from confusion to understanding. "Silver's what killed her?"

I nodded. "You mentioned before that you resisted your engagement to Jolene."

His brow wrinkled. "You're not seriously suggesting…" He placed his empty glass on the tray and I followed suit. It was good lemonade. Under different circumstances, I would have gone for a greedy second glass. It was a long walk home, though, and my bladder wasn't known for its patience.

"I want to prepare you, Alex, because the sheriff

may very well show up here tomorrow bright and early with a shiny pair of handcuffs. He's not exactly known for his thorough investigations."

He banged his fists on the porch ledge, nearly splintering the wood. "I wouldn't harm a hair on my mate's head. Jolene was everything to me."

"When?"

He looked at me and I noticed the golden sheen of his eyes. The great wolf was simmering just below the surface, ready to break out at a moment's notice. "When what?"

"When did she become everything to you? It wasn't before you got engaged. You said so yourself." Outwardly, I remained calm and cool. Inwardly, I was in meltdown mode.

He turned and leaned against the ledge. Better his butt there than his fists. "I hated the idea of being told what to do. I wanted to be free to choose my wife." He covered his face with his hands. "Jolene was a sweetheart from the very first day. It didn't matter that she was fighting her own demons. She still tried to be the best mate she could be."

"Was there someone else?" I asked. "For you?"

"Never," he snarled, and I jumped back a fraction. "It wasn't about another mate. It was about control."

That explained why he was heralded as a potential pack leader. Power and authority were ingrained in him, as natural to him as breathing.

"When did you know?"

I saw the hint of a smile. "It was the night of our engagement party. It was under the full moon." He stopped. "Pack rituals are almost always held under a full moon."

"Makes sense."

"After the ceremony, we turned together."

"What about the ordinance?" I asked.

"We can get special dispensation for events. It's called a limited license."

The bureaucracy in Spellbound never ceased to amaze me.

"You hadn't turned with her before?" I queried.

He shook his head. "It's not like that here. Turning with someone can be a very intimate experience." His expression turned wistful.

"What was she like?"

"Wonderful. Amazing." He smiled fully now, showing his teeth. "I'd thought of her as this docile, almost breakable female before that night. I couldn't imagine her as my mate. She changed my mind with one run through the forest."

"She liked her werewolf form?" I didn't know much about it. In the movies, it always looked like a painful transformation. The snapping of bones and stretching of skin. Yuck.

He rubbed the back of his neck. "Loved it. Jolene was truly herself in wolf form. When I glimpsed her raw energy that night..." He whistled. "I never looked at her the same again."

"I imagine it must have been difficult seeing her depressed," I said. "Especially when you knew she was capable of embracing life so completely."

His eyes softened. "It was soul crushing. Everything I did to support her, I did in the hope of seeing that Jolene again. The one from the forest."

I knew in my gut that Alex was innocent. Aside from his obvious love for Jolene, silver poisoning was a coward's tool and, by all accounts, Alex was no coward. I wasn't ready to end the conversation, though. Alex clearly needed to vent and I had the sense that his pack members weren't as willing to listen to him wax poetic about his beloved.

"Do you think she felt trapped in her human body?" I asked. "Maybe if she'd been able to turn more often, it would have helped to alleviate her depression?"

Alex shrugged. "It's possible. She was fighting her natural instinct and the wolf was strong in her."

"And everything she tried to do to combat those

feelings…" In my mind, I ran through the efforts she'd made—harp therapy, Daniel, potions. "They were all at odds with the state her body and mind wanted to embrace."

"But she didn't kill herself," he said firmly. "And I'd never…"

I held up a hand. "You don't need to tell me, Alex. I can see it in your eyes. Just be ready for Sheriff Hugo. I don't want to end up defending you in an official capacity."

He clapped me on the shoulder. "You're good people, Emma Hart. The pack is happy to have you in Spellbound."

"Give it time," I said. "I haven't been here very long."

CHAPTER 16

"I CAN'T BELIEVE you volunteered to host poker night in *my* house," Gareth complained.

"It's my house now, Gareth," I said. "If you don't want to observe the festivities, then go mope downstairs. I don't need your negative vibes ruining my fun."

He surveyed the room thoughtfully. "Which table are you planning to use?"

"The one in the dining room. It's huge."

He glided across the floor. "No, don't do that."

"Why not?"

"The living room is much better for entertaining. Bring the dining room table into the living room."

"With what? My super strength?" I asked. "I'm not a vampire, remember?"

"Haven't you learned any useful spells at the ASS

Academy? The devil knows you spend enough time there."

"I've learned plenty of useful spells. Blowback, the Shield spell, a transformation spell." And now I could add broomstick license to the list.

"Can any of those move a heavy wooden table from one room to another?"

I lowered my gaze. "No," I mumbled.

"Where's that useless angel?" Gareth asked. "I haven't seen him all day."

"I gave him the green light to go home," I said.

Gareth folded his arms across his chest. "Is that so?"

"I had it on good authority that the sheriff was turning his attention elsewhere." Plus, he'd been wearing the same outfit for days on end. It was time to change.

Gareth smirked. "I thought you might pretend the investigation was ongoing, just to keep him here."

"I didn't hide him here for my sake."

"Didn't you?"

I groaned in frustration. "We really need to find you other places to haunt."

"Send an owl to Demetrius for help," he urged. "I wouldn't mind watching his muscles at work."

"I can't shoot him down and then ask him for a favor."

"Sure you can. He's a vampire. He'll jump at the opportunity to prove his manliness."

"Is that how you were?" I asked.

"I had an ego, same as any other vampire."

I whistled for Sedgwick.

I'm not a dog," he said, immediately flying into the room. *You can just call my name.*

"I can call a dog by its name too."

How can I be of service, mistress?

"I need you to take a message to Demetrius Hunt."

That one again? I thought the bloom was off the rose.

"This isn't a love note. I need his help."

Then ask Daniel. He doesn't look at me like I'm his next meal.

"And neither does Demetrius." I scribbled a quick note and placed it in Sedgwick's beak. "No detours this time."

One time I decide to fly by the park and suddenly I have a detour problem.

"You get distracted by squirrels. I may have you tested for ADHD."

I don't know what that is, but I don't like the sound of it.

He flew out of the open window and I turned back to Gareth. "Okay, now what?"

"Get dressed," Gareth said. "Even if you don't want to date Demetrius, you have to look good when he gets here. Keep his interest."

"You sound like a 1950's housewife."

We retreated to Gareth's happy place—my closet. I began to change into a matching cardigan set and trousers.

"You can't wear that," Gareth said. "This is poker night. You look ready to head to court."

I studied my reflection. "What should I wear then? A tracksuit?"

His face contorted. "Have mercy, woman. Have you no sense of decency? No beachwear, sportswear, or fashion drudgery allowed."

"What qualifies as fashion drudgery?"

He swiveled his finger in front of me. "You're looking at it."

"Fine," I huffed. "How about this?" I pulled dark jeans and a brightly colored top out of the closet.

"Better, but you need accessories. There's a box downstairs in my closet."

"I cleared out the boxes."

"Not this one," he said. "You didn't see it, so I may have opted not to point it out to you."

I got changed and went downstairs to unearth the hidden box. Magpie ran ahead of me, as though eager to show me what I'd missed.

"Your cat is thumbing his nose at me," I said.

"Be grateful those are the only body parts he's using."

The box was pushed to the back of the shelf in the closet. It was filled with garish visors, a pack of cards, and a smaller box of magic cigars.

"How often did you play poker?" I asked. "The box is dusty."

"The country club hosts a Monte Carlo night every so often. And Lord Gilder would host the vampires on occasion. I didn't go as often as some of the others."

I placed a green visor on my head. "Do I look ready now?"

He tried to reach for a cigar, but his hand went right through the box. "Damn. I'll never get used to this."

"If I can get used to being a witch, then you can get used to being a ghost."

"Tell me who's coming tonight."

"No, let it be a surprise."

The doorbell rang. I whipped off the hat and Gareth disappeared to see who it was.

"Dem's here," he said, and I hurried upstairs to answer the door. "I just saw him smoothing back his hair on the porch. He wants to make a good impression."

"Doesn't everybody?"

I opened the front door and Sedgwick sailed in over my head.

Thanks ever so much, Sedgwick, he called, before flying upstairs.

"Your owl has an attitude," Demetrius said, smiling just enough to give me a glimpse of his fangs.

"Thanks for coming over on short notice," I said. "Do I need to invite you in or is that not really a thing?"

"You need to invite me in to be polite," Demetrius said. "But not because I'm a vampire."

With his snug black trousers and partially unbuttoned shirt, he looked too good to be in my house just to move a table.

"You look nice. Do you have plans?" I asked. Not that it was any of my business. If I didn't want to make plans with him, he should feel free to make plans with someone else.

"Are you asking?"

"No, sorry. I'm hosting poker night here. Ladies only." I gave an apologetic laugh.

"Then I should definitely stick around."

"Check out the way he's eyeing you," Gareth said. "My man is hoping for a reversal of fortune."

I tried to ignore Gareth. "I have a large table that needs to be moved into the living room. You were the first one who came to mind strong enough to move it." Okay, a little unnecessary flattery never hurt anyone.

"Not Daniel?" he queried.

"It doesn't need to be a competition, Demetrius."

He laughed. "Then you don't know the male species very well." He began to unbutton the rest of his shirt. For a moment, I was too distracted to speak. His pecs were...well, they belonged to someone more alive than undead.

"What are you doing?" I asked nervously.

He hung his shirt on the banister. "It's a neatly pressed white shirt. If I'm going to move furniture, I don't want to wrinkle it."

"Liar," Gareth said. "This is his peacock move. He's trying to catch your fancy."

"Well, it's working," I whispered.

"What's working?" Demetrius asked. Damn vampire hearing!

"Nothing," I said quickly. "The table is in the dining room. I'd like to move it to the living room."

Demetrius waltzed straight into the dining room, lifted the table with one muscular arm, and carried it into the living room like it was a handbag. He set down the table and grinned at me.

"Anything else?"

My mouth hung open. I was beginning to rethink my decision not to go out with him again.

The doorbell rang, jarring me back to reality.

"Company already?" Demetrius asked.

Gareth came gliding into the room. "You didn't tell me you invited Jemima."

"That's because I didn't invite her."

"Well, she's standing on our front porch wearing a hat that says 'girls allowed.'"

Great balls of fire.

Before I could make it to the door, she let herself in, just in time to see Demetrius buttoning up his shirt. I could see from her expression that she'd completely misjudged the situation.

"Hello Demetrius," she said, sliding a tongue over her upper lip.

"Good evening." He clearly didn't know her name.

"Demetrius, this is Jemima. She's in the coven and, apparently, she's here for poker night."

"I hope you don't mind," Jemima said, in a way that suggested she didn't care if I *did* mind. "I adore card games and I never get invited to any."

Gee, I couldn't imagine why not.

"I brought a bottle of Turtle Snaps." She thrust a green bottle into my hand. I had no idea what Turtle Snaps was, but my money was on alcohol.

"Be careful with that," Demetrius warned. "Don't make me send you another hangover remedy in the morning." He winked at me and Jemima nearly fainted.

When we'd gone to the Horned Owl together, I'd had too much to drink and he'd kindly sent over a hangover cure via owl in the morning.

"If you need anything else from me, you need only ask," Demetrius said. "I'm good for all kinds of chores. Unclogging pipes is a specialty."

"I'll keep that in mind. Thanks, Demetrius."

He flashed his fangs one more time before heading out the door.

Jemima gripped my arm, ready to yank it out of its socket. "Demetrius Hunt. Are you kidding? Why are you not upstairs with him right now instead of playing stupid card games?"

I wrenched my arm free. "I thought you adored card games."

The front door opened again and Lucy fluttered inside.

"I'm in it to win it, ya'll," she sang.

"Lucy, so glad you made it." I hugged her, careful not to crush her pink fairy wings. Lucy was one of the first residents I met in Spellbound. She worked as the assistant to Mayor Knightsbridge and was the best shopping companion in town.

"I wouldn't dream of missing a poker night." She noticed Jemima. "You look familiar, but I don't know your name."

"Jemima. I work at Mix-n-Match."

Lucy returned her attention to me. "Will I be the only non-witch in attendance this evening?"

"No, no. It's a healthy mix."

"Good." She fluttered around the room. "This house looks so much better. You've really done wonders here."

"Hey," Gareth objected.

"No offense to Gareth," she added.

Five minutes later and my house was filled with witches, a fairy, a vampire ghost, and a Valkyrie. I figured if tonight went well, then we could include other supernaturals next time. I was eager to meet

Althea's sisters, although I wasn't sure about three Gorgons in one room. One head of snakes seemed more than enough.

"Where's the creature from the deep?" Astrid asked.

"Gareth?" I queried.

"No, last time I checked, Gareth was dead. I mean that thing he claimed is a cat."

"Magpie's hiding. Crowds make him nervous," Gareth explained.

"He's hiding," I told Astrid. "He's not very social."

"Can I get anyone a drink?" I asked, once we were assembled in the living room. It occurred to me that I needed to improve my hostess skills. I didn't have any snacks or beverages out yet.

"It's all taken care of," Lucy said, waving her wand in the air.

A table appeared alongside the wall, covered in snack bowls and wine glasses. Jemima's bottle of Turtle Snaps was there, as well as a few other bottles.

"I think I called the wrong person for help earlier," I said.

"Never call a male to do a fairy's job," Lucy said.

"How did you know I called a male?" I asked.

"Do you think I didn't see Demetrius when I

arrived?" She wiggled her eyebrows. "He's hard to miss."

I went over to the table to pour myself a drink. Begonia sidled up next to me. "Why did you invite Jemima?"

"I didn't," I said softly. "She just showed up."

"And Demetrius?" she said. "Did he just show up too?"

"I needed him to move the table," I said.

Begonia fixed me with her hard stare. "I thought he was out of the picture."

"It was a favor. That's all." I took a sip of my drink and the bubbles tickled my nose. "You're not jealous, are you? You promised me you weren't."

"I'm not jealous," Begonia insisted. "Not exactly. But if you made it clear you're not interested, he may set his sights on another girl. That's all."

"Meaning you?"

She tasted a glass of fairy wine. "Only if I'm lucky."

I felt torn. On the one hand, I hadn't ruled out Demetrius completely. I just wasn't ready to dive into a relationship right now, not when I was still adjusting to this new life. Part of the problem was, of course, Daniel. It was silly, really. He didn't have a romantic interest in me, whereas Demetrius did.

And I *was* attracted to Demetrius. You'd have to be dead—truly dead—not to be attracted to the charismatic vampire.

"Begonia, other than with me, have you ever spoken with Demetrius?" I asked.

"Sure. Lots of times."

"I'm talking about more than 'thank you for holding the door'?"

She frowned. "Okay, no."

"You don't even know him. What makes you think he's the right guy for you?" I asked. "You know he has a certain reputation." Yet one more reason I was hesitant to get involved. I didn't want to be a conquest to him. Once he got his fangs in me, he'd be on to the next bare neck. Or so I'd been told.

"His reputation didn't stop you," Begonia said.

"It actually has," I said. "It's one of the reasons I'm hesitant to give him a chance."

"All right, ladies," Astrid said, placing an arm around each of us. "No more guy talk. It's poker time."

It occurred to me at some point during the evening that I should have learned how to play poker beforehand. My lack of skills didn't matter, though. Everyone was laughing and having a good time. The more I lost, the more everyone laughed. Like I said, good times.

The wind chimes alerted me to another guest. I hurried to the door to find Sheriff Hugo on my doorstep, his expression grim. Did someone complain about the noise? Maybe I should have invited the harpies after all.

"How can I help you, Sheriff Hugo?" I asked.

"Just wondering if Alex has been by your place tonight," he said.

"Alex?" I echoed. "No, why?"

"He's missing," the sheriff said. "And he knew I wanted to speak with him about Jolene's autopsy." He peered over my shoulder, picking up on the noise from the living room. "You sure he isn't here?"

"I'm afraid it's ladies only in here," I said, omitting Gareth. Somehow I doubted the sheriff would want to know about my invisible roommate. "I don't think Alex could pass as female no matter how hard he tried." The werewolf oozed masculinity.

"I went by his house, but nobody's there."

"Not even Kayla?" The younger werewolf always seemed to be around.

"Nope. No sign of activity." His subtle way of saying he peeked in the windows.

"Did you check his parents' house?" I asked.

"They haven't seen him since yesterday," the sheriff said.

"When I saw him last night, he didn't mention…" I stopped mid-sentence. Uh oh.

The sheriff squinted at me. "Where did you see him?"

"Um. Last night." I stalled for a split second, but it was no use. "At his house. I stopped by to see how he was coping."

Sheriff Hugo folded his arms and glared at me. "Did you now?"

"He seemed okay to me," I said. "Kayla made lemonade. It was delicious." No way was I elaborating on our conversation. The whole truth would get both Astrid and me in hot water.

He decided not to push the issue. "Send me a message by owl if you see him."

"Sure." I forced a smile, but my head was screaming.

Astrid appeared in the foyer. "Sheriff?"

The sheriff squinted. "Deputy? What are you doing here?"

Astrid ripped the visor with horns from her head. "Poker night."

"I see." Sheriff Hugo did not look impressed.

"Did I hear you say Alex is missing?" Astrid asked.

"That's right, but never mind," the sheriff said. "I take it you've been drinking."

"We've all been drinking," I said. "Except Laurel. She's been drinking lemon fizz."

"Then you should stay here," the sheriff said.

"Of course, Sheriff Hugo," I said. "We're having too much fun to leave."

As soon as he was out of earshot, Astrid bumped my arm. "We're not really staying here, are we?"

I flung my visor onto the steps. "Absolutely not."

"Good."

I strode back into the living room and clapped my hands. "Listen up, ladies. Alex is missing. Sheriff Hugo is searching for him. We're going to check the forest behind my house because it's a full moon and we know werewolves like to go there when they turn."

"But they're not supposed to turn," Lucy said.

"I know, but there's a chance Alex decided to do his own thing," I said. "Feel free to stay here and keep the party going. I'd like to look for Alex. Anyone who wants to join the hunt, feel free."

"What if he has turned?" Laurel asked. "Won't he be hunting us?"

"You stay here," I told her. "You're too young." To be fair, she was too young to be at poker night, but her parents seemed relaxed about her whereabouts. Maybe because she was the youngest of five.

"Everyone says I'm too young," Laurel complained.

Jemima grabbed her hand. "Stay here and play with me. I'm not going in the woods. I'm winning this hand."

Lucy fluttered nervously around the room. "Maybe I should send an owl to Mayor Knightsbridge."

"Why don't you wait until we have a better sense of the situation?" I suggested. "Otherwise, you'll upset her for no reason."

"Good point," Lucy said. "Then I'll stay here and keep playing."

Probably because Jemima was winning. Lucy seemed to be as competitive as I suspected.

"I'll come with you," Begonia said.

"Me too," Sophie added.

Millie glanced helplessly around the room. "Werewolves frighten me."

"But Alex is really nice," I said.

"Really nice werewolves don't kill their fiancées and then hide in the forest," Millie pointed out.

Although I wasn't convinced that was the situation, I was willing to reserve judgment.

"Okay, Astrid, Begonia, Sophie and I will head into the forest." Once I reached the foyer, I said to Gareth, "You keep an eye on the home front."

"Aye, aye, Cap'n," he said and saluted me.

I tucked my wand into the back of my waistband and headed into the woods with the other girls. Poker night just got serious.

CHAPTER 17

Leaves and twigs crunched beneath my feet. Thanks to the light spell, my wand doubled as a flashlight. It was a simple spell and very useful, especially now. The forest was so dark that I could only see about two steps in front of me. I suddenly felt foolish for insisting that we split up to cover more ground. We should have at least gone in pairs.

"Emma, is that you?" a voice whispered.

"Laurel?" I recognized her voice but couldn't see her. "I told you to stay at the house. You're too young to be out here."

"I know more spells than you do," Laurel said, appearing beside me. "Anyway, I didn't like the way Magpie was looking at me. His eye kept twitching."

"That's the way he always looks," I said. Like he's

ready to suck out your soul and feast on your innards.

"Well, I'd rather take my chances out here," Laurel said.

"Suit yourself. Just be quiet so we can listen." The forest was eerily silent. No birdsong. No leaves rustling. Not even the sound of scampering.

"What are we listening for?" Laurel asked.

"Anything to point us in the direction of Alex," I said.

"Do you think he's kidnapped Kayla to kill her, too?"

I spun around and faced her. "Where would you get an idea like that?"

Even in the darkness, I could see the embarrassed blush of her cheeks. "From Millie."

"Alex is not the killer," I said.

Laurel wasn't buying it. "How can you be so sure? You barely know him."

"Because not a single resident I've spoken to has referred to Alex as anything other than brave and a natural born leader. If he were going to kill someone, it would be swift and violent and he'd make damn sure everyone knew about it."

"If he's so brave, then why is he hiding out here?"

I didn't want to share my theory with Laurel. Not

yet. Like Linsey's case, I was fairly certain Jolene's death was about a guy. It was always about a guy.

"If Alex is out here, then I think it's for another reason. Now hush so I can listen."

We both stopped walking and listened intently for any sign of movement.

"It's as silent as the grave," Laurel whispered.

"Don't say that," I snapped.

"But it's true."

"Only if you don't commune with ghosts. The only reason Gareth's grave is silent is because he isn't in it."

"How's that going anyway?" she asked. "My mother says it must be a nightmare for you, having someone as critical as Gareth following you around all the time."

I glanced at her. "Your mother thinks Gareth is critical?"

Laurel immediately looked guilty. "I don't think she means to speak ill of the dead. We all adored Gareth."

"No, no." I waved my hand. "Do go on. I need ammunition for the next time he annoys the crap out of me."

"He had a certain way of doing things and he didn't like to be told otherwise." She hesitated. "They

259

served on the pet rescue committee together a few years back. My mom says that's when he adopted the cat."

"I would love to sit down and have a coffee with your mother one of these days," I said. I knew she was a witch and a botanist but little else.

Laurel beamed. "I'll let her know. Maybe I could come, too."

"Why do I get the impression you'll be there whether you're allowed or not?" It was difficult to bend the will of teenagers.

I heard a twig crack in the distance and placed a finger to my lips. Laurel nodded mutely. Of course, if we were dealing with a werewolf, it didn't matter how quiet we were. The wolf would've smelled us already.

"Oh," I said suddenly. A creepy yet strikingly beautiful white tree stood in front of me. "I recognize where we are."

I heard a noise from somewhere above. A low growl.

"That doesn't sound like a bird," Laurel said, glancing skyward.

"It isn't." I grabbed her by the shoulders. "Go back to the house and lock the door."

"Why? I want to come with you."

"It's too dangerous and I don't want to be responsible if anything happens to you."

"You need my wand," Laurel insisted.

Another growl. "I have my own wand. I need to go," I said. "Don't follow me."

I ran around the base of the white tree and pushed through the overgrown bushes. In front of me stood the hollow tree. It was too high for me to see the platform, but I knew that was where I would find Alex.

I climbed up the ladder as quickly as I could, oblivious to the growing distance between the ground and me. The empty bottle of Scorpion's Tail on the platform made sense to me now. When I reached the top, I took out my wand and prayed Alex was alone.

He was sprawled across the platform, trapped between shapes. Partially covered in fur with a human body and a wolf's head, it was like nothing I'd ever seen before. Judging from the contorted position of his body, he was in horrible pain. I had no idea what could have caused this, but one thing was perfectly clear—he hadn't done it to himself.

"Alex," I exclaimed and hurried to his side. It only occurred to me after I was beside him that he might lash out at me. Who knew what his mental state was in this condition?

He growled in response, but it wasn't an aggressive sound. More of a pathetic whine. Other than his in-between state, there were no obvious injuries.

"What are you doing here?" a voice asked. I didn't need to turn around to know it was Kayla.

"I heard his cry for help," I said, keeping my attention on Alex. "How can we fix him?"

I heard Kayla step toward me. We were far too close to the edge for my liking, but I couldn't make any sudden moves.

"He'll be fine," she said and crouched next to me. "I put a little something in his evening moonshine so that he could maintain a half-form. I heard it increases sexual pleasure."

What did she mean? Some kind of werewolf Viagra? I was almost too astounded to speak.

"Kayla, aren't you a little young to know about these things?"

"And aren't you a little naive? Listen new witch, just because you're destined to live a life as a spinster in some dead vampire's house doesn't mean the rest of us intend to go quietly into that good night."

Poetry? Who was this girl? "Are you telling me you and Alex are involved?"

"Not yet." She poked him in the furry abdomen with a finger. "I must have used too much of the potion. He's useless right now, but he'll shift back soon."

"Don't you think he's going to be upset with you for drugging him?" I asked.

"It'll blow over," she said, as though she'd borrowed his car without permission. "I'm all he has now and I'm the closest thing to his precious Jolene. He won't want to lose me."

I glared at the young werewolf. "So it *was* you." If she was about to kill me, I at least wanted to hear the truth from her first.

Her lips parted in an odd mixture of a snarl and a smile. "I would have preferred an old-fashioned fight to the death, but the pack doesn't follow dominance traditions anymore. A shame, really. I imagined ripping her heart out so many times, it would have been nice to actually do it."

Poor Jolene. I cast a sympathetic glance at Alex, still writhing on the platform. "Does he know?"

"No, and you're not going to tell him either. The dead can't speak, can they?"

Little did she know. "You want another death on your hands? Is that wise?"

"I heard you're afraid of heights." She peered over

the edge of the platform to the ground below. "Maybe you panicked and fell."

"The sheriff might find it suspicious that you were present at two recent crime scenes."

"Maybe, but he'll be so happy to be rid of you that he won't care."

Wow, saucy and insightful. I'd underestimated her.

Although I still clutched my wand, I had no idea how to protect myself. Kayla was strong and had the advantage of not being deathly afraid of heights. Thank goodness for the anti-anxiety potion. It was the only reason I hadn't had a complete meltdown already.

"Do you even know any spells?" Kayla challenged me. "I heard all you do is follow around the other remedial witches and ask stupid questions."

Kayla seemed to hear a lot of gossip for a teen werewolf that hung out in her cousin's house plotting murder and marriage.

"I know a few," I said, and extended my wand in her direction. "Care to test me?" Please say no.

She folded her arms and grinned. "Go on then. Try one."

Ugh. I'd successfully used the Blowback spell on

Mumford. If I managed it again, I'd send Kayla sailing over the edge to her death. Even though she seemed determined to kill me, I couldn't quite muster up the cold-bloodedness required to do the same to her.

She checked her imaginary watch and pretended to yawn. "Any day now."

Man, I hated teenagers.

I considered the other basic spells. One seemed better than the others under the circumstances. I focused my will and said the spell in my head so that Kayla didn't grasp my intention.

"You really do suck, don't you?" Kayla said.

I lowered my wand. "Guilty as charged."

She snarled and lunged for me. I stood perfectly still, watching as her face smashed against the invisible barrier I'd placed between us.

"You look like a pug," I said.

She banged her fists against the invisible wall. "What is this?"

I shrugged. "Sucky magic, apparently."

On the platform, Alex stirred. I noticed that his face now matched his body and the fur had receded. I also noticed that he was naked.

"Oh my," I said, and turned my head back to Kayla. "Why aren't you naked?"

"I'd like to be," she said. "But *someone* decided to interfere with my evening plans."

Alex raised his head and blinked. "Kayla?" His brow furrowed. "Emma?" He sat up and rubbed his temples. "What happened to me?"

"Long story," I said. "But the critical piece of information is that Kayla here is responsible for killing Jolene."

"Liar," Kayla said. "What a rotten accusation." To her credit, she managed to squeeze out a few tears.

Alex shifted his weight in order to stand and bumped against my force field. "What's going on?"

"I'm hiding behind this magical wall because Kayla wants to kill me."

"Because she murdered Jolene!"

It was so preposterous, I nearly laughed.

"Why would she kill Jolene?" Alex asked. "We only met her the day she came by the house, after Jolene was already dead."

Kayla was grasping at straws.

"Think about it, Alex," I said. "Kayla was the only one with access to Jolene that morning. She said she brought Jolene coffee every morning, probably laced with silver. She was the one who tried to pin the blame on Daniel from the beginning. Then she was eager to jump on the suicide bandwagon. The only

266

theory she wasn't willing to go along with was the one that pointed the finger at you."

Alex was clearly torn. He didn't want to believe that the young werewolf under his very own roof was responsible for such a heinous crime.

I felt the magical barrier dissolve a beat before Kayla did. She was fast but not as fast as Alex. He tackled her before she reached me and he pinned her to the platform.

So Kayla finally got what she wanted—Alex was naked on top of her. Somehow, I didn't think this was the scenario she had in mind.

Astrid appeared on the front of a broomstick, hovering beside the platform. "I heard you might need some help up here."

She hopped off the broomstick and I noticed Laurel still seated.

"You brought the deputy?" I asked.

"Obviously," Laurel shot back. "Sheriff Hugo is waiting at the bottom of the tree."

No surprise that she brought Astrid. Getting the centaur up a ladder or on a broomstick would prove difficult.

Astrid snapped open her handcuffs and moved toward Alex. "Get off the girl."

"Not Alex," I said. "It's Kayla you want."

Alex jumped to his feet and I heard Laurel gasp behind me.

"Cover your eyes," I told her.

"I can't," she said. "I'm on a broomstick. It's a requirement that we keep our eyes open."

"Then fly back down to the sheriff and tell him we're coming down," I said through gritted teeth.

Thankfully, Laurel did as she was told. I let Astrid lead Kayla down the ladder first. Not an easy task in handcuffs.

"Thanks for helping me," I said, once Alex and I were alone. "I wasn't sure if you'd believe me."

"It just didn't make sense that you'd hurt Jolene," he said. "Not that any of this makes sense. It's a nightmare."

"My house isn't far. Why don't you come back there and we can talk it through?"

"You might want to let me go down the ladder first," Alex said. "Unless you're interested in the view." He gestured to his private area that was on full display.

The back of my neck warmed. "Good thinking."

Everyone decided to converge back at my house, including the participants from poker night who'd apparently carried on playing after I left. The sheriff wanted to get a proper statement before transporting Kayla to a Spellbound holding cell and Alex wanted to hear what she had to say. I borrowed an outfit of Gareth's that I hadn't donated for Alex to wear, much to the vampire's dismay.

"He's been naked for hours. Surely he can stay naked just a wee bit longer," Gareth complained as I handed the buff werewolf a pair of leather trousers.

Alex slipped on the tight pants and Gareth gave him an admiring look. "On second thought, he can keep the trousers. They suit him better than they ever suited me."

"How generous of you," I said, watching Gareth stare at the werewolf's tight bottom.

"Is the vampire checking me out?" Alex asked. I'd warned him about Gareth's ghost the moment he entered the house.

"Don't take it personally. He offers a running commentary on everyone. You should hear what he has to say about Sheriff Hugo's bare hooves."

"If you're going to spread lies," Gareth complained, "at least make them good ones."

We rejoined the rest of the group in the living room, where Sheriff Hugo had just finished questioning Kayla. She didn't appear remotely apologetic or scared. A real sociopath.

"She totally confessed," Jemima said triumphantly, as though she'd single-handedly cracked the case from the comfort of my poker table.

Alex shook his head in disbelief. "So the silver in her body was from Kayla?"

"She brought her cousin coffee every morning," the sheriff explained. "At some point, she started adding a drop of silver. Just enough that Jolene wouldn't taste it. Over time, the poison built up in her system and killed her."

"Jolene took her coffee black and bitter," Alex said. "She was unlikely to taste it or smell it."

Kayla stood there, smug and defiant. "It was convenient. Milk and sugar would have made the whole thing more difficult."

"Why?" Alex asked, slapping both hands hard against the wall on either side of Kayla's head. "Jolene and I would have done anything for you."

"Not anything," Kayla spat. "She never would have willingly stepped aside. That depressed moron didn't deserve an esteemed place in the pack. She didn't have what it takes to be a leader." She puffed out her chest. "I do. I'm a wolf that can go the distance. Bring honor and glory to the pack."

"Honor and glory?" Alex repeated, baffled. "We live in Spellbound, Kayla. We lead pleasant, quiet lives. We're not asserting our dominance over a territory."

"Well, maybe we should," Kayla said, raising her chin a fraction. "And we should start with these ridiculous ordinances. No other creatures have the right to tell a werewolf when and where to shift. When you and I lead the pack, things will be different."

"When you and I...?" Alex flinched before stalking out of the room. He'd clearly had enough of her brand of crazy.

Did Kayla actually think she was going to walk free? Even crazier, did she think Alex would marry her?

"You poisoned Jolene slowly," the sheriff said, picking up the loose thread. "You didn't know when she'd drop dead, so you hung around waiting for the big day."

"Took longer than I thought," she admitted. "I was afraid the wedding would go ahead and then it would be harder for me." She bit her lip and fell silent.

"Didn't you realize the autopsy report would show the silver?" I asked. Even though she was a teenager, she seemed smart enough to register that fact.

"I figured they'd rule it a suicide. Or blame someone else."

"The way you tried to blame Daniel," I said.

Kayla flashed a diabolical smile. "Sorry about that. Didn't mean to drag your boyfriend into it, but with his history, he was an obvious choice."

"He's not my…" I stopped talking. My relationship status with Daniel hardly seemed important in this moment.

"Transport's outside, boss," Astrid said, peering out the window. "Looks like Mancini's here, too."

Someone must have alerted the head of the pack to the situation.

Lorenzo Mancini appeared in the living room. *My* living room. The house was beginning to feel like a public building.

Gareth whistled. "Nice suit."

Lorenzo didn't seem to own an ugly one. Each time I saw him, the aging werewolf looked more dapper than the last time.

"I understand you're conducting pack business without me," Lorenzo said. "I must say, Sheriff Hugo, this is terribly disappointing."

The sheriff grabbed Kayla's arm. "This is not

pack business. This is Spellbound business and the appropriate authorities are handling it."

Alex stood beside Lorenzo and placed a hand on his broad shoulder. "Let the sheriff deal with Kayla, sir."

Lorenzo gave his future replacement an understated nod. A sign of respect.

I stood by the front door and watched as Astrid joined Kayla in the deputy's jalopy. The centaur didn't need wheels when he had four hooves.

"It's so easy to lose your way," Gareth said.

"Especially when you're a psychopath."

Through the glass of the car window, Kayla's gaze met mine and I shivered. "Promise me something, Gareth. If I ever want to offer room and board to a friend, don't hold back if you think it's a bad idea."

He did his ghostly best to pat me on the arm. "I wouldn't dream of it."

CHAPTER 18

ONCE THE JALOPY PULLED AWAY, I returned to the living room where Lorenzo was busy grilling Alex.

"Kayla is guilty?" the pack leader asked. "You're certain?"

Alex's shoulders sagged. "We're certain. Even without her confession, the evidence points to Kayla."

"A waste of a good wolf," Lorenzo said. "And what happened this evening? How did you end up missing in the forest?"

Alex rubbed the back of his head. "I told Kayla I was going to turn tonight. I know there's the ordinance, but with all the stress over Jolene, my body was crying out to shift. I was willing to pay the fine. Kayla begged to come with me."

"But you told her no," Lorenzo said.

He punched his fist into his palm. "Damn straight. It wasn't appropriate. She's only a kid and Jolene's cousin to boot. Shifting with someone else is an intimate act."

In Kayla's warped teenaged mind, though, she viewed herself as an adult and a rival for Alex's affections.

"You didn't have any idea that she was in love with you?" I asked.

His dark eyes widened. "In love with me? Kayla?" Even now, he appeared oblivious. "I thought it was because she wanted to rise up the ranks and use me to do it. That she was tired of being treated like a cub."

I chose my words carefully. "Alex, I hate to be the one to lay it out for you like this, but Kayla wanted you and everything that came with being married to you. She murdered Jolene so that she could take her place in your heart and home. It's that simple." And that complicated.

A low moan escaped from Alex. A heart-wrenching, primal sound.

"You must have noticed something about her behavior," I said. "Flattery? Did she go out of her way to be around you?"

"She lived with us. It was hard not to be around

us." He raked a hand through his thick, wavy hair. "She always had a nice word to say to me. I thought she was just grateful for the room and board."

"Did you think she was going to live with you indefinitely?"

He looked completely blindsided. "I tried to convince her to go back to her parents, but she's a teenager. I thought it was only natural she'd prefer to live with Jolene and me. We weren't as strict as her parents."

"Was Jolene happy for her to stay?" I asked.

He opened his mouth to reply and then quickly thought better of his response. "At first, yes. She was always willing to help pack members in need. Plus, she was like a big sister to Kayla."

I could tell by the expression on his face that there was more to the story. "What changed?"

"Dunno. Jolene started talking about how great it would be when it was only the two of us again." He smiled wistfully. "To make room in the house for the cubs she hoped to have after the wedding."

Three daughters with horrible rhyming names. I already knew that part of the story.

"But you didn't associate her statement with a desire to get rid of Kayla?" I queried.

He shook his head. "Jolene wasn't that forthright.

In hindsight, I should have understood what she was trying to say."

I squeezed his shoulder. "It's not your fault, Alex."

"Isn't it? How could I have been so blind?"

"Speaking of blind..." Lorenzo made a noise at the back of his throat. "May I ask why you are wearing leather trousers?"

"Because he can," Gareth said.

Alex looked down at his tight pants. "It's either these or go all the way back to the Pines naked."

"Come along, Alex," Lorenzo said. "I shall save your dignity and take you home in my car."

"It will never feel like home again," he said. His pained expression seemed to underscore the remark.

Lorenzo shook my hand. Even his handshake felt expensive. "The pack is in your debt, Miss Hart."

"I'd rather not have anyone in my debt, Mr. Mancini."

"Nevertheless, if you find yourself in need of pack assistance for any reason, don't hesitate to send an owl."

Somehow I didn't think Sedgwick would be thrilled to fly into pack territory on my behalf.

At this point, everyone had cleared out of my house with the exception of Jemima. Since I hadn't wanted her at poker night in the first place, it was a mystery as to why she was lingering behind.

"How could he not know?" Jemima asked, scooping up a handful of snacks and munching away. "There's no way they could spend that much time together for him to be clueless about her feelings. He probably liked the attention. Those werewolves like their egos stroked as much as their fur."

My thoughts immediately turned to Daniel. I knew exactly how easy it was to fall for someone without the other person realizing it. Not that I'd go so far as to admit I was in love with him. I preferred to think of it as a case of extreme like.

"Secrets are all too easy to keep, I'm afraid," Gareth said, gliding around Jemima. "Take it from someone who knows."

"She can't hear you, remember?" I said.

"I know. I said it for your benefit." He gave me a knowing look.

"Is that Gareth?" Jemima asked, scrunching her nose and peering around the room like she was hunting down a fly on the wall.

"The one and only," I said.

"Awesome. Can you do me a teeny favor and ask him if my butt looks big in this dress?" She stood and turned, flashing her derriere in our direction.

"Why would you need to ask Gareth?" I asked. "I can tell you." That the answer was a firm yes.

"Because he's a gay male. They have the right opinions on these matters."

I scratched my head and looked at Gareth, who simply shrugged. "I can't decide whether to be flattered or offended," he said.

"I don't want women to make a habit of coming over here to see if their butts look big," I said. "I don't live in a public mirror."

"I won't tell anyone. So what's the verdict?" she asked, patting her behind.

"It's fine," Gareth said with complete disinterest. "Very flattering."

"He says it looks like two cats fighting in a trashcan."

"What?" she and Gareth said in unison.

I made an apologetic face. "Sorry. He's very blunt. Must be the Scottish ancestry."

Jemima made an unpleasant squeal before spinning on her heel and marching out of the house.

I pretended to dust off my hands. "That should nip any future unwelcome visits in the bud."

Gareth gave me an appraising look. "You really do have a tough streak," he said. "I like this side of you."

"Better than looking at the backside of *her*." I jerked my thumb toward the front door.

"Can we do poker night again next week?" he asked. "It's the most excitement this house has seen in ages."

I surveyed the disaster in the living room. Poker chips scattered everywhere. Dirty wine glasses. "I don't know if my heart can take it."

He followed my gaze. "No worries about the mess. That's what your fairy cleaning service is for."

I thought about Alex and the mess his life was now, all because he and Jolene trusted the wrong person. It was a huge risk—placing your faith in another person.

The next morning, Gareth swept into the kitchen, gesticulating wildly. If he weren't incorporeal, I'd worry he'd knock something over.

"Daniel's here," he said. "Quick, magic yourself a brush and do something about that rat's nest you call a hairdo."

Instinctively, my hand flew up and touched my hair. "I don't know how to do spells like that yet."

"No wonder you're in the remedial class," he grumbled.

"Cut me some slack," I said, incensed. "I passed my broomstick class, didn't I?"

The doorbell chimed.

"I miss my organ bell," Gareth said.

I shrugged. "Too bad. I changed it. New owner's prerogative." I opened the door to greet Daniel. As always, my heart caught in my throat at the sight of him. I wondered if that feeling would ever go away. Knowing that he was committed to a romance-free lifestyle, part of me wished it would. For my own sanity.

"Hi," he said. "Are you busy?"

"She was just about to get naked and roll around in a tub of whipped cream," Gareth said.

If I could make contact with Gareth's shin, I would have kicked him. "Not at all. Come in."

Daniel stepped into the foyer. "I heard you hosted an eventful poker night."

"I did." No surprise that word got around. Word seemed to get around when a tree fell in the woods and no one heard it.

"Maybe next time you'd think about inviting me," he said.

"You'd want to come?" I was so flabbergasted, I didn't even remember to say that it was females only.

ANNABEL CHASE

"I like card games. I used to play a lot." He hesitated. "I suppose it was quite a long time ago, but still."

"Then I'll be sure to let you know next time." I hardly thought the women of Spellbound would object to ogling Daniel under their green visors all night.

"Now that you're here," I said. "I have something for you."

"Really?"

I hurried to the kitchen counter where I'd left the stack of Winnie the Pooh books. Magpie was standing on top of the pile like he was claiming them.

"Scoot, Magpie," I ordered.

He hissed before leaping to the floor. Maybe he wanted me to read to him. Stranger things have happened.

I brought the books to the foyer where Daniel was waiting. "For you. Well, temporarily for you. They're from the library."

He read the covers. "So this is a Winnie the Pooh?"

"Read them in your thinking spot," I said. "I think you'll enjoy the stories. There's a character called Eeyore you might relate to."

He grinned. "As it happens, I have a present for you, too."

"Another one?" He'd already given me the blue and yellow pot on the living room mantel.

"This one's better. You need to come outside."

My present was outside? "Okay." I said with exaggerated slowness.

"Oh wow," Gareth said. "You're not going to believe what it is."

"Don't ruin it," I snapped.

Daniel glanced at me. "How would I ruin it?"

I softened my tone. "Sorry. Not you."

"Gareth?"

I nodded and stepped onto the front porch. In the driveway sat my green 1988 Volvo.

"Sigmund," I cried. I couldn't believe it. The last I saw of Sigmund, my beloved car was being swallowed by Swan Lake. "How did you manage it?"

Daniel beamed. "It wasn't easy. I needed help from a few strong dwarves and one inventive elf."

"Quinty?" I'd heard about Quinty's engineering prowess.

He nodded. "Quinty fixed it so that it runs on magic like the rest of the cars here."

I threw my arms around his neck and hugged him tightly, trying to ignore the feel of his taut muscles beneath the thin layer of clothing. "Thank you so much, Daniel."

"It's nothing," he said, disentangling from me. "Just a show of gratitude for helping me to avoid Sheriff Hugo."

I hopped down the steps and hurried over to caress my car. "I never thought I'd see you again," I murmured.

"It was rusted from the lake, so the elves gave it a fresh coat of fairy paint and replaced all the necessary parts with magical ones."

"No more walking all the way to town," I said happily.

"And you don't need to ride a broom if you don't want to," Daniel added. "I know how you feel about heights." He opened the driver's side door and gestured for me to enter. "Let's take it for a spin."

Gareth sat beside me in the passenger seat. "Where do you think you're going?" I asked.

"I want to go for a ride," he said.

I jerked my thumb. "Out."

Daniel opened the passenger door and sat down just as Gareth disappeared. "Do you know what to do?"

I studied the dashboard. It was both familiar and mind-boggling. "Not a clue."

He grinned and my insides melted. "Hit that button there." He pointed to a red button on the steering wheel.

"Are you sure about this?" I asked, my finger hovering over the button. "You said you weren't suicidal anymore."

"I trust you."

I hit the button and my heart soared along with the magical engine.

We drove into town, past the impressive fountain designed by the naiads. Past the town square and the clock tower. Past the charming shops and restaurants. I tried to take in every detail from this new perspective without running anyone over.

"Sigmund has never run so well," I said. "It's like he's had a transplant of all his internal organs."

His sensual mouth quirked. "And that's a good thing?"

"He was on his last legs," I said. "I just didn't want to admit it because this car was the last physical connection to my grandmother. To my family." Tears pricked the backs of my eyes. "I miss them every day."

Daniel reached over and patted my thigh. "They'd be really proud of you."

I hoped so. "Thank you. This is the best present you could have given me."

"I'm glad."

I cast a sidelong glance at him. "Am I part of your redemption package or something? You do enough nice things for me and your halo returns?"

His pleased expression faded. "You think I have an ulterior motive?"

No, but I wanted him to. "You're going out of your way for me and you hardly know me."

"I know it's strange to say, but I feel like I've known you forever."

I smiled. "Yeah. Me too."

That was the thing about Spellbound—forever wasn't much of an exaggeration.

I returned to the house an hour later, elated.

"Did you see my car?" I asked Gareth.

"You know I did."

"Isn't it wonderful?" I spun around the room.

"I think you mean isn't *he* wonderful?"

"Don't ruin the moment, Gareth. Let me enjoy it."

"Go ahead and enjoy it, but just remember—the car is an act of kindness, not a promise to love you for eternity."

I placed my hands on my hips. "Hey, that reminds

me. What about *your* promise? The big secret you promised to reveal?"

Gareth feigned innocence. "What secret?"

"I've passed my broomstick class," I said. "You owe me one Spellbound secret."

"Well remembered, Emma." Gareth smiled, showing his ghostly fangs. "Do you know what Lady Weatherby's given name is?"

I thought for a moment. "J.R., isn't it?"

"And what does J.R. stand for?"

I shrugged. "Jacqueline Rose?"

"Jacinda Ruth." He paused. "If you really want to annoy her, call her by her childhood nickname—Cindy Ruth. She absolutely detests it."

Somehow, Cindy Ruth wasn't nearly as intimidating as Lady Weatherby. "Thanks, Gareth. I can work with that." It was like picturing the audience naked during a public speech. The name humanized her.

"You're welcome. Use it wisely."

I cocked my head and studied him.

"What?" he asked warily. "What's that look? It has a rather saccharine quality to it."

"I really want to hug you right now, but you're too intangible."

"Thank the devil for small favors."

"I mean it, Gareth. I don't know what I'd do without you. I'm so glad you're in my life."

I felt a gentle breeze caress my skin as he reached out to touch my cheek. "And I'm so glad you're in my death."

I laughed. "Do you want to sit in my car and pretend to go for a drive?" I figured as long as we stayed in the driveway, Gareth wouldn't disappear.

"I'd love to. You can tell me about your grandmother," he said. "I want to know everything there is to know about Walnut Grove. All the juicy details."

"Lemon Grove," I corrected him. "And I'll tell you every boring detail." Because I trusted him. It was a huge risk, placing my faith in someone else, but I decided it was one I was willing to take.

* * *

Thank you for reading **Doom and Broom**! If you enjoyed it, please help other readers find this book ~

1. Write a review and post it on Amazon.

2. Sign up for my new releases via e-mail here http://eepurl.com/ctYNzf or like me on Facebook so you can find out about the next book before it's even available.

3. Look out for *Spell's Bells* and *Lucky Charm*, the next two books in the series!

Made in the USA
Coppell, TX
26 January 2023

11758016R00164